Love on Call

Nantucket Romantic Comedies, Volume 3

Taryn Daniels

Published by TD Books, 2024.

LOVE ON CALL

First edition. June 21, 2024.

Copyright © 2024 Taryn Daniels.

ISBN: 978-1763585126

Written by Taryn Daniels.

Chapter 1

CLAY

As I step onto the Nantucket ferry, I sense this family vacation will test my patience, sanity, and ability to keep up with a five-year-old hurricane named Rex. I'm the fish out of water, a single amongst three married couples and a hyperactive kid.

I feel like an imposter—I am a pediatric surgeon who works with children every day in and day out, but little Rex manages to exhaust me within ten minutes of being in his presence.

My brother, Liam, claps a hand on my shoulder, his excitement pumping like he's ready to play his next NBA game. "Can you believe it, bro? A whole week on Nantucket with this crew. We're gonna have the time of our lives."

I muster a smile. "Yeah, it's going to be great." A poor attempt to sound enthusiastic.

Trina, my optimistic sister-in-law, ruffles my hair. "Come on. You can do better than that, Clay. You're going to love it. Who knows. Maybe you'll meet someone special on the island."

I chuckle, my face heating up. I'm not the only one who notices I'm the single in the group. All of Trina's sisters hold Nantucket dear to their heart. That's where they fell in love with their soulmates. Well, that's not going to be my story. I'm just happy to have time off work. This trip is an opportunity for me to unwind and let go of my workaholic tendencies.

My knee gives way from a karate kick from behind. "Whoa." I windmill my arm and steady myself.

A blur of Rex dodges between the crowd.

"Hey, dude," I call after him.

Liam laughs. "When does that kid run out of energy?"

I shake my head. "I should've brought my anesthetist so Rex could have a solid nap"

"Aw," Trina croons. "He's only a little excited."

"A little? Gee. Wouldn't want to see him on Christmas morning."

"I thought you loved kids?" Trina asks like the journalist she is.

I tunnel my fingers through my windblown hair. "I do."

The sun casts diamonds over the ripples of the water's surface. The ferry's horn announces our departure. I take a deep breath of the salty sea air. This trip is all about family bonding. I'm not here to focus on my career or my everlasting single status.

"I'll go find Rex and win him over. Maybe then he'll stop playing kick and run."

Liam grins. "Looks like he's adopted you as an uncle. A good kick to the shin is his sign of affection."

I'm surprised Dalton hasn't sorted Rex out. Bet little Rex has his stepdad wrapped around his finger. The kid has a contagious giggle so you can't stay mad at him long. Even though I probably have six bruises by now.

I pass Melanie, Trina's younger sister, and her husband, Adam, who are busy taking selfies against the picturesque ocean backdrop. Melanie pokes her head to one side. "Clay." She waves for me to come.

Oh, no. She wants me to feel included. I don't need to photobomb them reminiscing about their honeymoon on Nantucket.

I shove my hands in my jeans pockets and make my way toward the shiny rail beside them.

Melanie holds out her phone. "Can you take a picture of us?"

Looks like I'm not only an adopted uncle/babysitter but a couple photographer too. "Sure."

I take her cell and snap a few shots. As I'm about to hand back Melanie's phone, another familiar voice calls out.

"Wait a minute." Pam squeezes in next to her sister. "Get one of us too." Her husband, Dalton is right behind her.

I look around for Rex. Aren't they worried about their son?

As if Pam can read my mind, she points. "He's fine. Talking that granny's ear off."

I spot him and it's true. The white-haired woman is bent over nodding and smiling away at Rex.

Liam and Trina join the party and now all three couples squeeze together, smiling for the camera, their faces bathed in the warm sunlight.

I crack a genuine grin. I may be the odd one out, but through my brother's marrying into Trina's family, our family has tripled overnight. I love these people.

The harbor is dotted with sailboats and the sky is painted in shades of deep blue. Maybe, this trip to Nantucket, with its charming cobblestone streets and historic cottages, promises a perfect escape from my hectic life on the mainland.

AN HOUR LATER, WE'RE rolling our luggage down a winding path toward our accommodation. Roses of pink, white and yellow pop from the gardens that line the pavement. Their scent mingles with the salt air. That, with the sound of the crashing waves in the distance, makes me instantly relax. No wonder the Smith girls wanted to come back here. Melanie and Adam's anniversary falls a week after Pam and Dalton's. Trina and Liam live on the MA coast and didn't want to miss out. Liam dragged me along saying I needed a vacation.

"Ah. Brings back memories." Adam sighs. He looks at his wife. "What about you? Do you remember much of it?"

I scrunch my nose. What does he mean by that? It was their honeymoon.

Melanie laughs. "I remember hiding behind the bushes over there with a knife in my tote bag."

"What?" I jerk my head back. "Am I missing something here?"

My brother laughs. "If you thought Trina and I had a rough start to marriage, wait til you hear their story. It's crazy."

Adam circles his temple with his forefinger. "Next level crazy."

Melanie swats his hand. "I had amnesia. I wasn't crazy."

He shrugs. "Lost your mind. Crazy. Same thing when you're running all over Nantucket in your PJs claiming your husband kidnapped you."

My cheeks fill with air, and I burst out laughing. "Oh boy. Can't wait to hear the full story."

"It's a riot," Dalton says as he lowers Rex to the ground and takes his hand. "We all have fond memories here but also some we want to forget." He gives Pam a wink.

Ahead of us is a wooden sign, a little askew with faded paint stating, *Reception.*

"Let's check in, shall we? You all can fill me in on your stories by the pool." I flap my shirt to my chest. "I'm breaking out in a sweat in this heat."

I roll my luggage to the door and as soon as I step inside the office, air conditioning hits my cheeks. Ah. Just what the doctor ordered.

The reception is filled with pastel colors, soft and soothing. A curved server counter with a high-backed chair remains empty, but there's a silver bell. One wall is lined with a library of colorful brochures, and to the side is a small coffee table with a vase of fresh cut roses.

I ring the bell and by habit push the handle of my bag into place as I wait. My newly extended family pour into the cramped space behind me.

A young woman emerges from a narrow corridor, likely where the caretaker lives. She's wearing denim cut-offs and a white button-down shirt that is rolled up at the sleeves and tied into a knot just above her midriff. I guess since this is an island, everyone dresses casual.

"Hey. Let me get my aunt. She's around here somewhere." The woman smiles as she passes me and circles the others to go outside.

She cups her hands around her mouth and yells, "Marg! You've got guests to check in." She makes her way back inside and disappears down the same corridor.

I look at Liam and scratch my chin. My frown says, *What is this place?*

He gives a slight shake to his head as if it's nothing. *Chill out, Clay.*

Liam knows I'm a bit of a snob when it comes to accommodation. I work hard so I like to stay in five-star establishments. Dalton would be the same. He's a successful businessman. But family life seems to have worked its magic on him. By his relaxed expression, he's happy to be here.

A gray-haired woman comes from around the corner. Must be Marg.

Her face brightens when she sees Adam and Melanie. "Ah! You all made it back." She engulfs Melanie in a hug. "I was thrilled when I saw your reservation." Marg swivels on her heel to face Trina. "I watched the whole season of *Bride at First Sight*." She claps her hands in front of her chest. "I knew you'd win." Marg pats Liam's cheek. "And I knew you'd win Trina over. Not an easy task, but you did it."

Marg steps back and holds her hand out to Rex. "Hey, little man. I remember you." After shaking his hand, she straightens and stares Dalton in the eye. "Is he still running rings around you both?"

Dalton chuckles. "You bet. We brought our own cyclone to wreak havoc on Nantucket. Hope you've weather-proofed the place."

She nods. "The unit you're staying in is child-proof. But I won't put anything past this guy."

Marg makes her way behind the counter and scans the computer screen in front of her, typing in a few commands. "You'll be staying in unit three, the apartment with a view of the ocean. It's perfect for a family your size."

Marg takes a key off a hook and hands it to Dalton. "Now let me get you a map of the island, just in case you've forgotten your way around." She winks at Melanie. "You'll need one too, no doubt." Marg turns her back to us and rummages through a drawer.

Okay, so I get why the others wanted to come back to this place. Marg is warm and friendly. She's like the grandmother I never had. I like her.

As she turns with a stack of glossy folded maps in her hand, she startles when she sees me. "Oh, forgive me for being rude. I haven't introduced myself. I'm Marg." Her brows angle inward. "This is your first time at the Rose Resort?"

"Yes, ma'am." I gesture to the outside. "Nice place you have here."

Marg checks her computer screen. "You must be Clay Ashley."

"You must be right."

She smirks and folds her arms across her chest. "A smart man, I see. What do you do for a living, Clay?"

Trina steps up beside me. "He's a pediatric surgeon. Pretty darn smart, I'd say." She nudges me with her hip.

Marg side-eyes me. "Are you single?"

Liam barks a laugh.

I drop my chin. I'm a little speechless right now.

Marg goes bug-eyed when she must realize how that sounded. She tsks and waves a hand. "I'm not asking for me."

I look at Dalton. I bet he used to get this a lot when he was single. Once older women find out you're loaded, they're trying to match you up with their daughter.

"Did you meet my niece earlier?"

I frown. Does she mean the staff member whose idea of greeting guests is yelling down the garden path to get the manager?

Marg points over her shoulder toward the corridor. "I could introduce you."

I grit out a smile. "I'm good, thanks. Can't wait to jump in that pool. What unit am I staying in?" I lift my gaze toward the computer, hoping she gets the hint.

Marg smiles and settles into the high back swivel chair. "Certainly. I'll check you all in. One jiffy."

Chapter 2

KAT

What in the world is going on outside? I peek through the office window and frown at the group laughing and playing by the pool. They stand all huddled up like a team ready to hit the court, their expressions eager. What is it about them that low key irritates me?

One of the women grabs a man by the arm and they leave the pool area, heading down the path that leads to the beach. The woman stops and leans in close to smell the roses, her eyes alight with laughter when the guy says something into her ear. She plucks a rose and twirls it between her thumb and forefinger.

"Aunt Marg won't like that. Not supposed to take the roses." I'll have to make sure she adds another sign to the fence. Ugh. Great. I'm getting as bad as my nosy older neighbor when I lived on the mainland. I swear that woman called if she noticed I stayed up later than usual or left my kitchen light on past ten pm.

I'm not normally this annoyed at guests doing what guests do, but I'm not gonna lie, it's been a heck of a day and I'm over it. "Must be nice to take a vacation and spend all your time by the pool." I grumble and yank the curtain back over the window.

"Did you say something, dear?" Aunt Marg breezes into the kitchen, humming one of her favorite tunes. "Is something wrong?"

I shake my head even though her back is to me. "Nope. Just being grumpy."

"Oh dear. Is your computer giving you trouble again?" Marg's white hair curls around her head in a bright halo that makes her look like the angel she is.

"It's fine." It's not, but I can't keep complaining to my aunt about my laptop woes. It's my own fault for not upgrading when I took on the medical billing and coding work on top of my admin position. "Are those for the guests?"

The air conditioner chugs hard to pump cold air into the kitchen and I shift closer to the vent to catch a breeze before heading back to the office to finish out my day. I came to the resort for a change of scenery while I worked. Now I'm thinking I would've been better off staying in my unit down the path.

Aunt Marg scoots a flaky strawberry danish to the edge of the tray. "Oh, shoot. Looks like that one isn't going to fit. Mind taking care of that for me, dear?"

I can't help laughing at her obvious excuse to get me to eat one of Ellie's scrumptious treats. I'm also not going to pass up the chance for a bite of sugar. I grab the pastry and shove it into my mouth. "You're the best."

She waves me off with a flick of her hand and lifts the tray to her hip.

"Let me take those to the guests for you." It's the least I can do to help out since Marg is letting me kick up my heels in her kitchen while she works. Maybe stepping out into the sunshine will cure my bad mood. I gobble up the last bit of pastry and wash my hands before reaching for the tray. If it was just me, I'd lick my fingers clean. But Aunt Marg would have my head if I handled her guests' food with dirty hands.

She releases the tray all too easily and brushes her hands together. "Well, if you're sure you don't mind. I need to check on Steve and get ready for tomorrow's guests."

Before I can remind her that Uncle Steve is on the water with Samantha and won't be back until dinner, she's disappeared.

Huh. That's odd. If there's one thing my aunt loves, it's chatting. I'd halfway expected her to be my biggest problem and distraction from getting my work done today.

A childish scream rips through the air, followed by a massive splash. I yank my entire body around in time to see a little boy doggie paddling over to the edge of the pool. He drags himself out of the water and takes off running around the pool. A wild mix of nausea and fear cramps my stomach around the pastry.

Where are his parents?

Gripping the tray with one hand, I yank open the sliding door and hurry toward the pool. The boy never stops his headlong rush as he aims at the pool and jumps.

"Hey," my voice is lost in another huge splash as the kid cannonballs directly into the pool.

Bright sunlight reflects off the pool and blinds me. My foot catches on the edge of a lounge chair and I stumble several steps before regaining my balance. That was close. I drop the tray onto the closest table before it ends up in the pool and look around for an adult.

The little boy paddles around the pool, grinning from ear to ear. Straight across from him, a large white sign covered in black lettering spells out the rules for the pool.

Number one is no running.

Number two is no diving or cannonballing into the pool.

I glare from the kid to the sign and back again. He's too young to know how to read, so I can't blame him for his actions.

His parents, however, are perfectly capable of reading and making sure their kid obeys the rules. They're there for a reason. One injury is all it would take, not just to get the pool shut down but for the kind of agony I can only imagine as a parent. The mere thought of a kid getting hurt out here sends terror spiking through my heart.

I keep one eye on the boy and have every intention of stopping him if he decides to make another run around the pool. For now, he's content paddling back and forth. Sweat gathers on my forehead and trickles down my nose. I swipe it away and tap my foot while I wait for an adult to show up.

A man's voice trickles out from behind the wall that separates the main pool from the sauna and showers. I latch onto the space and wait with a sort of eager anticipation as the man's voice rises in pitch, then falls low. He sounds annoyed as he ends the call and finally steps into view.

The sight of him almost makes me forget why I'm out here, but the boy's laughter reminds me and gives me a sense of fierce satisfaction as I stomp across the concrete and point at him. "What do you think you're doing?"

He steps between two lounge chairs and looks around, his eyes wide and his brow furrowed. "Me?"

"Yes, you." I motion at the pool. "You can't leave your kid unattended." I slam my hands onto my hips.

"I—"

I cut off his excuse with a slash of my hand through the air. "Don't you dare say you didn't." My eyes narrow and I give him a look that would make a lesser man take off running. "I've been standing here for five minutes while he swam alone. You were nowhere to be found."

"Well." He rubs the back of his neck, pink tinging his cheeks. The move causes the muscles in his chest and arms to flex.

And he's not wearing a shirt. Yikes. Now my face is hot and there's no doubt I'm red as a tomato. It's not like I don't see guys shirtless all the time. I mean, hello. I live on Nantucket, where people barely bother throwing on anything that isn't beach ready. Something about seeing him bare chested is different. I can't put my finger on it, but it takes way too much effort to drag my gaze away from the toned muscles. Even though he's so pale he's already getting sunburned, the guy is ridiculously fit.

It's an image I'll have trouble getting out of my head, but his looks are not important. Not when he leaves his kid alone in the pool.

"The rules are right there," I say while jerking my chin toward the sign. "He's been running *and* doing cannonballs into the water. Do you have any idea how dangerous that is?"

"Uh, yeah, actually, I do." His voice is solemn, matching the dark brown eyes and flat lips that look like they haven't smiled in years.

Do not feel guilty, Kat. I give myself a firm peptalk and barrel ahead. It's nothing to do with me if the guy hasn't found anything to smile about. Maybe he should spend more time with his kid and not on his phone.

We glare at each other for a full five seconds before I harrumph and shake my head. "Make sure you read and follow the rules. He's too young to be out here alone. You're lucky I saw him and came outside."

The guy looks around as though he's searching for someone, anyone. Well, there's no one out here to take responsibility for his mistake except him.

Splashing water has us both spinning toward the pool.

"Watch me." The boy heaves his little body out of the pool and gets ready to bolt.

"Rex, stop." The guy holds up his hand in a stopping motion, and the kid looks at him with his mouth puckered. "It's not safe to run, okay. Or jump in the water. You could get hurt."

He looks at me with an expression that looks like he's seeking my approval. I don't give it to him. I did what I came out here to do. "Aunt Marg wanted me to bring out some snacks. They're on the table." I motion toward the tray and spin around, more than ready to get back to work now that I've averted certain disaster.

Man and boy fuss behind me. The boy—Rex—insists that he's being careful, and I lose track of the guy's words as I step into the house and close the door firmly behind me. I catch one last glimpse of them before I walk away.

Matching heads of dark hair lean toward each other. The man whose name I didn't bother to learn, motions toward the sign and the boy frowns. He must be explaining the rules.

Good, and not a moment too soon. It should have been the first thing on his mind when they arrived at the pool, not whatever the phone call was about.

His actions scream workaholic. Nothing gets in the way of his work. Why is he even here if he's not going to leave his work behind? I roll my eyes and head toward the reception area. It's none of my business.

"Did you meet the new guests?" Aunt Marg stands from her chair and rushes over.

I start at the sight of her. "I thought you were looking for Uncle Steve?"

She waves off my question. "He's still out with Samantha. You know how those two are. Once they start talking about boats, they'll be out until dark." She drags a second chair over to the desk and motions for me to sit. "Keep me company for a bit."

"I should get back to work." The urge to call it a day is fierce. I'm caught up on recent billing and really all I'd be doing for the next two hours is trying to get the spreadsheet updated. It's nothing that can't wait until tomorrow.

Funny how I was just harping on the guy about responsibility and now I'm contemplating playing hooky for the rest of the day. It's different for me. I'm not putting a kid at risk.

"I'm so glad Melanie and Adam came back." Marg's eyes gleam as she rubs her hands together and laughs. "I wish you'd been here that week. Oh we had such a good time."

Her steady chatter keeps me from having to respond, but when she brings up the boy, Rex, I tune back into the conversation.

"That boy, I tell you. He's going to be so much fun. He's a handful. Pam and Dalton sure are going to be busy keeping up with his energy."

I sink my teeth into my lip to keep from telling her that I caught Rex doing cannonballs into the pool. She'd worry, and I don't want to put any additional stress on her.

"Liam brought his brother this time." Marg continues. "He certainly seems nice."

"That's good." It really is. I like when nice people stay here. It makes life easier and it helps Marg and Steve keep the resort going. "I should head out."

I know Aunt Marg well enough after all these years to recognize when she's up to something. Now is one of those times. Her eyes practically dance with that inner light of mischief. It always means she's sticking her nose in her kids' business. I might not be her child, but I'm her niece, and as far as Marg is concerned, that's excuse enough to deep-dive into my life too. I'm not sure what's going on this time, but it's time for me to go.

"Oh." Marg snaps her fingers and reaches behind the computer. "Before I forget, Ellie left a message for you. She said she called your phone but didn't get an answer."

The slip of paper is a leftover scrap from an old brochure, and Marg's pretty handwriting covers the image of the lighthouse. I tilt the paper to get a better look at the words. "She needs me to work the bakery tomorrow? I can't bake."

"Just keep an eye on the front." Marg doesn't look at me but turns her attention to the windows stretching across the front of the reception area. The ocean glitters in the distance, the soft crashing of waves beckoning me to stick my feet in the cool water. I never get tired of this place. Getting to come back here after my annulment was the biggest blessing of my life.

Pain shoots through me at the reminder of my failed marriage. It wasn't fair that the man I'd loved lied to me about his condition. It wasn't until he turned violent and possessive that I knew something was wrong and finally learned the truth.

A shudder wracks my spine. I hope he's getting the help he needs.

Chapter 3

CLAY

My empty stomach grumbles at the tantalizing aroma of freshly baked pastries when I step into *Sweet by Design*. I've been tasked with collecting breakfast for our hungry crew. The bakery buzzes with customers, and I'm greeted by the sight of Marg's boisterous niece behind the counter. Oh, man. Is she going to blast my eardrum again?

She manages a polite smile when she sees me, a stark contrast to our heated exchange at the resort pool yesterday. I'd been trying to juggle a phone call and didn't realize I was the one left to keep an eye on Rex as he enthusiastically performed his cannonballs. Understandably she was concerned about resort rules and safety and assumed I was Rex's dad. The woman sure didn't hold back in giving me a piece of her mind.

I approach the server, determined to mend the awkward encounter. "Morning," I attempt to sound cheerful despite the memory of our clash. "I'd like to order some breakfast, please."

She nods, her expression composed. "Of course. What can I get for you today?"

I glance at the display of pastries and inhale the scent of baked bread. "Let's see... I'll have seven croissants, a couple of cinnamon rolls, two blueberry muffins, two strawberry..." I tap my chin. "... and three orange and poppyseed muffins to go."

She begins assembling my order, her hands moving swiftly. "Any drinks with that?"

I smile, relieved that the tension seems to have eased. "I'll grab a coffee for myself. I'm not a fan of the instant back at the resort."

As she prepares my order, I shift on my feet before breaking the ice. "By the way, I wanted to apologize for yesterday," I say, my voice sincere.

"I didn't get a chance to explain, but I'm not Rex's dad. I got an urgent call from the hospital."

She glances up from her task, her jaw dropping. "Oh, was everything all right?"

"I'm a doctor. A nurse had some follow-up questions for one of my patients. Usually, they don't call me when I'm on vacation. But in this case, I'm glad I took the call."

She swipes her arm across her forehead, leaving a smudge of flour. She looks even cuter up close, her green eyes captivating.

"I shouldn't have come to conclusions without asking anything," she murmurs. "Where were his parents?"

"Pam must've gone off to the unit and trusted that I was able to babysit Rex for a few minutes. He knows how to swim pretty well. Pam brags how he's been taking lessons since he was a baby."

"Mm. Except for reading lessons so he can figure out the pool rules." She grins sheepishly. "Just kidding. Sorry for going all school principal on you."

I nod, grateful for her understanding. "No worries. It was a crazy moment. By the way, I'm Clay."

"I'm Kat. Nice to meet you, Clay." She places a lid on my coffee and hands it over with the rest of the order.

I take the breakfast bags and tap my card on the machine. "Thanks." I lift my paper cup.

Kat leans on one hip. "So, what kind of doctor are you, Clay?"

"I'm a pediatric surgeon."

She raises an eyebrow. "A surgeon? Makes sense why you had to answer the call."

I nod. "Yeah, sometimes work takes over, even on vacation."

Kat smiles warmly. "I understand the industry. I'm a remote admin assistant for a medical firm."

I'm intrigued. "That's interesting. And it's totally cool that you can work from Nantucket."

She peeks over her shoulder, perhaps checking if her boss needs her, before answering. "A lot of people are doing it this way these days. I'm staying at the Rose Resort with my aunt. My parents own the unit I'm living in. Thought I'd take a break from the hustle of the city."

"Wish I could do the same. You're fortunate to have that option." I peer into the kitchen area. "And you work here as well?"

"Oh, no. I'm helping my cousin. Her hubby is sick, and she has a wedding cake order. She'll pay me in doughnuts and coffee."

"Nice." I stare at the smear of flour on her forehead. Should I tell her?

Kat scrunches her nose and touches her head, brushing more flour into her bangs. "Do I have something on my face?"

My ears go hot. It's a weird thing that happens to me when I get embarrassed. It doesn't happen much. Not since high school, like when I tried to talk to a pretty girl or ask them on a date. This is not that situation, and I'm thirty-six now. I should be over it. Hopefully, my ears aren't blazing red.

I gesture to her hair. "Looks like flour."

"Thanks for letting me know." She laughs and fluffs out her bangs. "Is it gone now?"

I lean across the counter and brush the spot above her brow. As soon as my fingers touch Kat's skin, an electric sensation shoots up my arm, sending goosebumps all over my body.

"Now it has." I swallow hard.

Kat's eyes go wide for a moment. We're both frozen in place, staring at each other.

"Thanks." Her voice comes out like a breath. She clears her throat and steps back, averting her gaze. "I—I better keep working." She turns around and moves on to serve another customer.

I stand there dazed, trying to make sense of what happened. This is ridiculous. I'm a grown man, not a lovesick teenager. But the way

Kat looked at me just now, the way her skin felt under my touch, that electric zap . . . it's like nothing that's ever happened to me before.

I shake my head and force myself to focus. I grab the breakfast bags and coffee and head out of the bakery. The morning air is cool and refreshing from yesterday's heat, and I take a deep breath to clear my head.

As I cross the street, someone calls my name. "Clay. Hey, Clay, wait up."

It's Adam. The Australian in our group. "Thought you might need a hand." He points to the bags.

"I'm managing okay. But thanks for the offer."

"I also came to get some of Ellie's cookies. Melanie remembered the oatmeal ones she had here and pretty much demanded that I buy all of them."

I chuckle. "She's not pregnant, is she?"

His eyes go wide. "I don't know. Is that a symptom?"

"Demanding her husband buy the shop's stock of her favorite treats might be a sign."

"Oh, man. That could explain a few things."

KAT

I'm tempted to lock the door behind Clay and go home to bury my head under the covers. I made such a fool of myself yesterday. I mean, I was right to make sure Rex didn't get hurt, but accusing Clay like that was not my best moment.

I blame the stress and anxiety that ate up six months of my life last year. A groan slips out. I grip the edge of the counter and roll my head from side to side.

"Could I get another of those blueberry muffins?" An older woman taps her fingernail against the glass pane separating her from her tasty treat. Her fingertip leaves a smudge that I'll have to clean up later. A groan tightens my throat. It's basic human nature to tap the glass, but I really wish people understood how hard Ellie works—and me when I'm helping out—to keep the glass spotless.

Focus. I need to focus on getting this job done and helping Ellie. "Here you are, Mrs. Wilson." My smile is tight as I slide the muffin over and take her money in return.

A harried-looking man rushes through the door. "You have any of those oatmeal cookies?"

I recognize him from the group who checked into the resort yesterday. "Sure." I fish one of the chewy oatmeal cookies from the tray.

"I need all of them." He rubs his hands together and swallows hard. "My wife wants all of them."

"No problem." I've filled weirder requests. This one isn't even top ten on the levels of strange I've encountered. "Would you like anything else with them? Clay didn't take any drinks." I hesitate before continuing. "Sorry, I didn't catch your name."

"Adam." He scans the room quickly before shaking his head. "Nothing to drink. Thank you."

"Here you go." I eye the stack of cookies. "Twenty-two oatmeal cookies." The scent of oatmeal and sugar fills my nose and I brush the back of my hand over my forehead, remembering Clay's touch earlier. My face fills with heat at the memory. I've been in and out of the kitchen all morning. I probably look awful. Humidity and my hair are a guaranteed recipe for disaster. I blow a breath straight up into my bangs. What do I care if Clay saw me with wild hair and flour on my face?

"Thanks." Adam slides his card, takes the bag, and is out the door with another thanks and a wave, taking off like his life depends on getting those cookies back to his wife.

Mrs. Wilson chuckles from her seat a few feet away. The chatter from her and her friends has been a nice reprieve from my own chaotic thoughts today. I never mind helping Ellie out, and it's not just because of the free sweets.

"I'm almost done." Ellie sticks her head out of the back where she's been working all morning on finalizing the wedding cake. "You okay?"

"Yep." Playing with cookie aesthetics is way easier than managing medical data. I love my job, though. "You're almost out of muffins, and Adam just took all the oatmeal cookies."

"Melanie must be reliving her honeymoon." Ellie chuckles and tips her head toward the front door. "I'll take over in a little bit."

"Take your time." I'd much rather stick around at the bakery than risk making a fool of myself around Clay again. Which is exactly what will happen if I run into him at the resort.

I can't believe I acted that way yesterday. No wonder he looked uncomfortable when he walked in and then when he apologized. I feel like a fool, but it doesn't really matter. Clay and

his family will be gone soon, and I'll never see them again.

All for the best, really. When I think about Clay and the shadows in his eyes, I remember why I don't do relationships. Love is not happening for me. Not ever again.

"You want to see it?" Ellie asks. She motions for me to join her in the kitchen. "Come on. If anyone needs anything, they'll ring the bell."

The Joneses and their bells. I roll my eyes at her but follow my cousin into the spacious kitchen. Flour floats in the air, creating a sparkling haze that reminds me of cotton candy. The air smells sweet and fresh from the cakes and other delicious treats.

I stagger to a stop as my mouth pops open when I catch sight of the cake Ellie has been working on all day. "Whoa."

"I know, right?" Ellie claps her hands, sending up a plume of flour. No. I taste the air. Not flour. Powdered sugar.

I walk around the counter and eye the cake from every side. Ellie deserves the praise, and it's easy to give it. "This is amazing. You sure you don't want to go on one of those baking shows?"

Ellie's laughter is quick and light. "No way. I get enough excitement here without all that added TV drama. Just watching Liam and Trina's reality TV show had my heart pumping."

"Who and what now?" I scrunch my nose. "Why do I feel like I should know those names?"

"Trina and Liam." Ellie waves a hand, sending another puff of powdered sugar up into the air. She must have been using it to keep the fondant from sticking to her hands. "They came here for their honeymoon. Mom about had a fit when the producers told her what they were up to. Then they ended up actually falling in love. It was so sweet."

"Wait, Liam Ashley." The names I saw on the computer screen when I booked a reservation for someone yesterday finally made sense. "Clay Ashley."

Ellie's grin grew into a full-blown smile. "Aren't they adorable? Mom says she'd never have known they were brothers until she saw them goofing off at the pool together."

The mention of the pool causes my face to heat again. I may never live down that moment where I blasted Clay. I feel like I owe him more of an apology, but since I plan on staying away from him, it's really not necessary. He can enjoy his vacation and hopefully lose a little of that bleakness from his eyes.

"Why don't you go home?" Ellie grips my elbow, tugging my attention back to her face. "I can handle the front now that I'm done with the cake."

"You don't need to deliver it or anything?" I give the cake another long look. Ellie really has outdone herself with this one. The four tiers are perfectly proportioned and balanced against each other. White fondant roses start at the bottom and climb each tier, ending in a cascade at the top where a pop of matching red roses represent the bride and groom.

Ellie shakes her head. "Nope. They're getting married nearby and having the reception at the church across the street. It'll be no problem to carry it over when it's time." She pats the wheeled cart where the cake sits. "That's the whole reason I bought this thing."

I can't deny that I'd love to spend some time on the beach today. I've been back on Nantucket for a while but I've been so wound up that I spend all my time working.

And I called Clay a workaholic. The thought makes up my mind for me. Time to get out and enjoy some Nantucket beach therapy. Sunshine and waves, that's what I need.

Chapter 4

Yep. This is exactly what the doctor ordered. The thought causes a quick giggle to escape. I shield my eyes from the sun rippling off the water and relax on the sand. I should have gone home to change first, but the impromptu trip to the beach was too good to pass up. It's not the first time I've washed sand out of my denim shorts.

A couple strolls past, laughing and shoving each other. The woman pushes the man into the surf and he goes down with a splash, only to come up seconds later laughing and spluttering.

He grabs the woman around the waist and hauls her in amid her laughing protests.

This is the place I love most, with the wind in my hair and well, not the sand in my shorts, but all the rest. I wiggle around to a sitting position and grab my phone. It's been forever since I shared anything on my social media. Things spiraled after my annulment, and I wanted to avoid the spotlight for a while. Not that I have a following or anything, but it is nice to have these memories to look back on. It's time I started living my life to the fullest, and I'm going to document this moment with a live video. Standing, I brush sand from my legs so they won't itch and adjust my hat so it's propped on the back of my head.

It only takes a few seconds to get the video rolling. I angle the camera toward my face and raise it so I'm in the best possible position. My smile is genuine and carefree for the first time in way too long. I wave at the camera and point over my shoulder. "I used to think that retail therapy was the best thing in the world. Turns out that sunshine and ocean waves beat new shoes. At least, it does for me."

I move the camera around so I'm only taking up half the video and the ocean waves crash in the other half. A man appears in the distance, but the sunlight is so bright that I'm sure no one will pay him much attention. He focuses on the ground near his feet, stooping occasionally to pick up something from the sand.

"Life isn't just making it from moment to moment." I point over my shoulder. "This is what life's all about." It's not until I squint against the sun's glare that I realize I pointed right at the man on the beach. Another quick peek over my shoulder and I realize that the man I just pointed at is Clay.

Oof. My face flames hotter than the sun. I quickly end the video, consider erasing it, but ultimately decide against it. Who's going to care anyway?

My cousin, Tim, maybe. I can't help grinning as I imagine Tim seeing the video. He's such a big brother when it comes to me and guys. No doubt he'll call the minute he sees it. If he does. He's been so busy with his lawyer practice and being newly married that he probably doesn't do much browsing on social media anymore.

My grin falters as I remember our last chat, right after my annulment. Tim really helped me through it all. The hardest part of my life, and it was my grumpy cousin who made me feel validated and safe.

"Kat?" Clay's smooth voice carries on the wind.

Drat. He found me. Not that I'm hiding. Not by any means. For goodness sake, I'm standing on the beach in broad daylight. I tuck my phone into my pocket as I turn and paste on a smile. "Hey, Clay." I tent a hand over my eyes and look past him. "No Rex today?"

"He's with his parents." Clay chuckles dryly. "I'd offer to bring him to the beach, but I'd probably need one of those kid leashes that parents use at theme parks sometimes. That kid has some crazy energy."

I can't help grinning at the look of amusement on Clay's face. He doesn't seem to mind Rex's rambunctiousness. "He's a cute kid."

"Yeah." He scrubs a hand along the back of his neck and brushes away sand. "Seems weird that I've only known him a few months."

"Oh?" Curiosity nibbles at me. This is my chance to learn more about them as a whole family. The dynamics are tight, and they all seem to get along. But I know how easy it is for some to hide their pain and the mental turmoil. Tim fooled them all for years with his gruff attitude and downright meanness. He used it to push them all away so he couldn't get hurt again.

Clay shrugs one shoulder. "You mind walking with me? I left my shoes on the path and my feet are burning up."

Hmm. Am I curious enough to take a walk with the cute doctor? He hops from foot to foot, and I take mercy on him. "Yeah, sure."

His sigh of relief makes me grin. I hide my smile and case into a slow walk along the water's edge. "So?"

Clay angles his head toward me while staring out over the water. "You sure you want to hear all this?"

"Trust me, I love learning about families." It's true. I love family dynamics and how they play off each other. It's something I never got from Danny. His name scorches through me like hot lava. I wince at the force of it.

Danny. Groan. I should've known better than to marry him so quickly. It was what my mom called a whirlwind romance. It was a whirlwind all right. We were married and then not married within six months. He shattered my trust in men and in myself. I don't know when I'll manage to trust anyone again. It feels like everyone is hiding something nowadays. And I can't stop worrying that I'll be made a fool of again. Getting close to anyone feels impossible.

Clay drags his feet along the wet sand, carving trenches and grinning. "Quick version is that my brother married Trina during one of those reality TV shows. It turned into real love and they're happily ever after newlyweds now. I first met Rex, Trina's nephew, during one of the competitions that the show set up."

This is the quick version? I nod as I listen, keeping the people sorted in my head requiring most of my thinking. I'm grateful for the reprieve from thoughts of Danny.

"What was the deal with the oatmeal cookies?" I pull my hair over my shoulder to keep the wind from snarling it into knots and turn toward the white fence that eventually leads to our units.

Clay laughs outright and scratches again at his neck. "Oh, that." Merriment twinkles in his eyes. "I told Adam that Melanie might be pregnant because she sent him to the bakery with orders to buy out all of Ellie's oatmeal cookies."

My own laughter bursts out. "You did not." I can't believe this guy. He's all serious and stern on the outside, but I sense there's more than meets the eye underneath.

His eyes crinkle at the corners, creating little lines that tug on my heart. He's really kind of adorable, in a sexy, doctor way. I'm not making any sense, even to myself.

"I'm not even ashamed. Not after that little hijinx at the pool where they left me alone with Rex." He shakes his head. "Did you know that kid has been up at daylight every single day begging to go swimming?"

"Yep." I twirl a finger around and tap my ear. "I hear him running past my unit on his way to the pool."

A wrinkle of confusion creases his brows, but a shout in the distance brings both our heads up before I can explain that I'm usually up and already at work before dawn. I mentally called Clay a workaholic, but it seems I might be headed toward the same path. I do get things wrapped up pretty early in the day though.

Most of my afternoons are spent near the water, with the occasional trip out on one of Samantha's catamarans.

"Let me go." A young voice wails and Clay and I barely glance at each other before we both take off at a dead run. My heart drums hard in my chest. Sand sprays behind me, peppering the backs of my legs with heat.

Clay surges ahead of me and reaches the path first. It's too narrow for me to come alongside him, so I'm forced to stay behind.

Annoyance clenches my hands into fists, and I slip to the side and try to look around him. Long arms pump in time with his strides. The man was built for running.

"Mooooooooom." The annoyed boy's voice slices the air.

Clay rounds a corner in the path and comes to a sliding stop in the shade of the last unit at Rose Resort. The soft fragrance of Marg's roses linger though it's well past midday. Ocean winds cause the roses to wave at us, but it's the sight on the porch one unit down that has my mouth dropping open.

Rex flails up and down in a man's arms, flopping like a fish. I vaguely recognize him, but I look to Clay before I accuse the man of attempted kidnapping. The story about Mel and Adam has been told at Marg and Steve's dinner table often enough that I know it by heart. I'd rather not be the one chasing after the guy, but I will.

Clay appears amused instead of concerned, so I relax. "What's happening?"

Clay glances over his shoulder. "Your guess is as good as mine."

"But Rex is okay?" I can't help asking for clarification.

He reaches over and flicks his thumb over my cheek, brushing away grains of sand that scrape my skin. "Dalton is Rex's stepdad. That's the guy holding him right now. I'm assuming he's fine."

"Rex seems to have a different idea of what fine means," I say when Rex lets out another bellow.

A woman appears from down the other side of the path, a bottle in one hand and a towel in the other. She points the bottle at Rex. "I told you, young man. No going to the beach without sunscreen. You're already getting sunburned."

"Busted." Clay's laughter tumbles out and the sound winds around my insides, loosening knots I didn't even know were there.

I poke his shoulder, where a line of red creeps down past his sleeve. "You should listen to her advice, or I'll be calling you Doctor Lobster."

Rex kicks his feet up and down, the motion throwing him against Dalton's arms. "I don't wanna wear sunscreen. It's itchy."

I snort out a laugh and shake my head at the kid while raising a brow at Clay. "Well? Are you going to do anything?"

He takes a step back and raises his hands. "Nope. Not my circus. Wrangling Rex is worse than herding cats. And I deal with kids on a daily basis." His eyes do that crinkling thing again.

Eh, excuse me, what now? It takes a second for my brain to catch up to the memory that he's a pediatric surgeon. I nudge him with my hip. "Yeah, but that's because all your kids are under anaesthetic when you see them."

"Hey, not all the time." His laughter deepens until his shoulders shake. "Okay, most of the time. But I do see them before and after surgeries. And their parents. And let me tell you, there is nothing scarier than a worried parent."

Something pinches in my chest as I take in the look in Clay's eyes. He loves his job, that much is obvious from the way he smiles. But it's more than that. He's at ease with himself and his career, and when he talks about his job, he lights up.

When was the last time I was that passionate about anything? Since before Danny, that's for sure. I don't like that Danny has that much influence over my life even now. I've moved on from that phase of my life and I'm still working on putting it fully behind me.

Coming back to Nantucket was part of the moving on process. Seeing my family whole and healthy and learning that Tim and Nathan—my twin cousins—are mending their own pasts, has given me a chance to discover that wounds do heal. They take time, but I'm willing to give myself all the time I need.

Marg keeps pushing for me to get back out there, but what's the point? I fell in love once and it was a disaster. I'm in no hurry to repeat the process.

Rex and his parents are still fussing in the background, and I drag my thoughts back to the situation. I approach Rex and put on a happy smile. "Hey, Rex."

He stops long enough to glance at me. His eyes widen and I know then that he remembers me from the day at the pool.

I stop a few feet away and put my hands on my hips. "They forgot to tell you the secret about the sunscreen."

"Secret?" He flops over to look at Dalton. "What secret?"

I cup my hands around my mouth and look around, making a big show of making sure no one overhears. "The reason the sunscreen is so sticky is because it has super powers."

His mouth pops open and he wiggles upright. "Can it make me fly?"

Oh boy. I didn't think this through. Rex is the kind of kid who will take everything to the extreme.

I frown and give my head a slow shake. "No flying. But it makes you run super fast. It might even make you invisible." I whisper the last bit.

"I want to try it." He reaches for his mom and grabs for the bottle. "Use lots of it. I want to be invisible."

The woman mouths "thank you" at me while slathering sunscreen on Rex's back and shoulders.

Clay gives me an appreciative look. "That was quick thinking." He leans in close, meeting my eyes. "But I'll only wear sunscreen if it gives me superpowers too."

"Oh, it would give you powers all right." I scoff at him and wave a hand toward the ocean. "It'll make it so you can stay in the sunlight without turning beet red and getting stuck indoors for the rest of your trip." I shield my eyes from the sun and turn away from Clay.

His laughter follows me, and I'm tempted to ask him if he needs help with his sunscreen. Wouldn't that be a sight? Me smearing sunscreen across Clay's broad shoulders and down his back.

My face flames. I'm glad he can't see me as I hurry away. Clay Ashley is not good for me. He makes me want things that I gave up after my annulment. I'm supposed to focus on myself, on what I need. And I do *not* need a handsome man like Clay messing up my carefully planned life of singleness.

Chapter 5

CLAY

Jogging on the beach of Nantucket is far superior to running on a treadmill. The scenery alone is enough to make it worthwhile. My feet thud steadily against the sand in time with my heart's rhythm, and the breeze plays with my hair while cooling the sweat beading down my spine.

After a long stretch of beach, the heat of the sun and the occasional sprint causes my muscles to burn. Time to cool off.

I slow my steps, tug my shirt over my head, and throw it to the sand. In three strides, I dive under the first small wave that comes my way. Refreshing cold hits my torso, and I let the waves carry me for a few moments. I break through the surface with a splash, blinking away droplets from my eyes.

The sight before me is picturesque—sailboat masts bob in the distance pointing to the sun, and the vibrant colors of the vessels contrast with the turquoise water. Simply stunning.

I swim several strokes until I'm close enough to grab onto a buoy moored along a pier. With one arm hooked around it, I float on my back, taking in every detail of this small slice of paradise.

And people like Kat get to live here. I'd love to get a beach shack or something on Nantucket. Visit on the weekends. That would be the balance I need in my life. It can't be all work and no play.

I flip over and swim back toward the shore. Soon enough, there's sand beneath my feet again, and I trudge out of the sea, invigorated and energized.

I haven't brought a towel with me as I didn't plan on swimming, but it's a short stroll to the resort. I collect my shirt from the sand and make my way to the accommodation, taking in deep breaths to regain my oxygen levels after the intensity of the swim to shore.

The scent of roses wraps around me as I climb the stairs to my unit. Just as I'm on the last step, Kat comes out of the apartment next to mine. How convenient. Did Marg purposely give me the unit next to Kat?

Kat startles when she looks up and nearly drops her manilla folder. "Oh, hi, Clay." Her gaze travels over my bare chest before meeting my eyes. Pretty pink flushes her cheeks.

I wipe my damp hair with my shirt. I wasn't going to get it wet, but with Kat blushing over there, I reconsider and shove my shirt on in one swift move.

"Hey, how are you?"

She places both hands on her folder in front of her and rocks on her heels. "Good. And yourself?"

"Great. I would jog and swim at that beach every morning for the rest of my life if I could. This place is a slice of heaven."

Her teeth gleam. "I practically grew up here. Every school break, my parents would take us to Nantucket. This is my home away from home."

"Where's home usually?"

She shifts on her feet. "Nowhere at the moment. I'm taking one day at a time. Needed some space from the mainland. It'll be hard to return."

A grunt comes from the bottom of the stairs. I turn and a scowling man stomps toward us, his steely glare set on Kat.

I look over my shoulder to find Kat's face pale as a sheet.

"Is everything okay?" I step closer to her.

She covers her mouth. "It's my ex. What's he doing here?"

Her ex? I take a step back, giving her space. "Do you want me to stay?"

She bobs her head and tries to steady her breathing.

He reaches us, and his eyes flicker over me before jerking back to her.

"What are you doing on Nantucket, Kat?" His tone is low and threatening.

"I'm staying with family for a few days." She tries to sound casual, but I can tell she's scared. This is not the Kat I first met at the pool who was bold and sure.

"Kat. Come on. You can't keep running away from me. We need to talk about this."

"Nothing to talk about." Her voice is strong, but her grip on the folder trembles.

"I don't want to do this in public." He glances at me before advancing.

I step in front of Kat, shielding her from him. "Is there a problem here?" I ask in a no-nonsense tone.

He glowers at me. "This doesn't concern you. Mind your own business."

"I believe it does since you're making Kat feel uncomfortable."

Kat's ex scoffs. "Right. Like you're her hero or something."

"I'm not looking to be a hero. I'm just trying to make sure everyone is safe," I state calmly.

He huffs and turns to Kat. "We need to talk."

"I have nothing more to say to you," Kat's voice wobbles and the sound does something to my insides.

"We'll talk whether you want to or not." He grabs her arm.

I slap my hand over his and remove its hold from Kat. "You need to leave."

He tries to pull away, but I hold firm.

"Let go of me, you—" He spits out a string of expletives.

I tighten my grip. "I suggest you leave before I call the police."

He sneers at me, but finally steps back.

Then his eyes go wide, and his head snaps back. "You're the guy in the video."

I look to Kat for some info. What's he talking about?

"Are you moving in on my wife?" He raises his voice.

Wife?

"I'm not your anything, Danny." She inches closer to me like my presence is giving her the confidence to stand up to Danny. "We had an annulment as if we were never married."

Annulment? What on earth went on for the court to approve an annulment?

Danny grumbles. "Who is this guy? Are you sharing a room with him?"

I step in between Kat and Danny and straighten to my full height. "Look, man. Kat has made it clear that she doesn't want to talk to you. Whatever you had with her before is over. She's moved on and you need to move on too." I gesture to the exit path of the resort.

Danny puffs out his chest and locks eyes with me. "Tell me this one thing and I'll go. Are you seeing Kat?"

I never shift my gaze from his and add conviction to my tone. "Yes. And I won't leave her side. You can't cause her pain anymore." I keep my voice level.

Danny grits his teeth and without another word pivots, jogs down the stairs, and disappears out of sight.

Kat crumples to the ground, gasping for air.

I kneel next to her. "Are you okay?"

She frantically nods and bats away my hand when I reach for hers. "I'm fine. I just need a moment."

I back off and wait for her to compose herself.

Wow. So that is Kat's ex. He's the reason why she's on Nantucket, running away. And he's the reason a woman full of confidence and strength can, in an instant, fall into a heap of nerves. Poor woman. What happened in their marriage for her to react like this?

I sit beside her and place a comforting arm around Kat. This time she lets me. I pull her closer, and she rests her head on my shoulder.

"Thanks," she whispers. "I'm glad you were here."

"Good thing your aunt gave me the unit next door."

She manages a laugh. "Yes, very convenient indeed."

We remain silent for a long minute, before I ask, "What did he mean by the guy in the video?"

"On my social media. I posted a live video, and for a second, you were in the background. It's frustrating that I can't get completely free from Danny. When will it end? I've blocked him on everything. Now he's discovered I'm here and came looking for me. I don't think he has the mental capacity to understand it's truly over. He's locked onto the idea that he owns me or something. It's weird."

"Danny looks like some hard wires have short-circuited. Can I ask how you ended up with a guy like that?"

She gives a self-deprecating laugh. "He was all charming in the beginning. A perfect gentleman. Told me only after a few dates that he was so in love with me and wanted me to become the mother of his children." Kat shakes her head. "He was so infatuated. I don't know why I didn't see the red flags. He proposed three months after we met and two months later convinced me to elope rather than spend thousands on a wedding."

"Whoa. That's quick. Maybe he wanted to marry you before you realized what he was really like."

Kat jumps back an inch and faces me. "Exactly. He didn't tell me he had borderline personality disorder. And he wasn't doing any therapy to improve his mental health. If I'd known how volatile he could be, I wouldn't have rushed into things."

"Ah. So that's why the court approved the annulment. Makes sense now."

"I didn't know before we got married, but he knew his diagnosis. We were only married for six months. It took most of that time to get out." Her gaze snaps toward the stairs. "But in his mind, it's not over. When will he let me be free?"

"Do you think he's going to leave Nantucket?"

Her lips twitch. "I doubt it. He knows where I am . . ."

"You need to get a restraining order."

She takes a deep breath and cups her face. "Oh, that will be a last resort. The guy has enough problems as it is. It's not his fault he has BPD."

I frown. I see it as two different things. She needs to be safe, no matter what. Danny is responsible for getting the help he needs. Kat needs to protect her own mental health. Living in fear of Danny showing up at any moment is going to affect her. The way she was shaking earlier is proof that it has already taken its toll.

I gently lift Kat's chin and lock eyes. "I told Danny I wouldn't leave your side. If he's here on Nantucket, he won't get a chance to get to you."

She gives me a small smile. "You don't have to do that. You're on vacation."

I tuck a strand of her hair behind her ear. "I want to be here for you. Make sure you're safe."

A tear pools on her lower eyelid and she pulls away, fidgeting with her fingers. "Thanks." Kat collects the papers that had scattered to the ground.

I help her and we slip the forms back into the folder together.

"I have so much work to do." She straightens and pushes her shoulders back. "I'll work in Steve and Marg's house. I'll be fine there."

I nod. "I'll walk you."

As we make our way through the resort, I look at her with newfound respect. Despite everything that's happened, she's still able to hold her head up high. I've only known her for a few days, but already I feel more protective than I ever have before for anyone. It's not my place to tell Kat what to do, but maybe she needs someone who'll be there for her.

We arrive at her aunt's place, and Kat walks inside without saying anything. I follow her in and watch as she puts her stuff down on the kitchen table and organizes her papers.

"Are you going to be okay here?" I ask.

She peeks up at me and nods. "I'll be fine."

"Okay. Well, I'll come check up on you later."

"Sure." Her voice is soft.

As I turn to leave, she calls out, "Wait."

I swing around.

Kat walks up to me, goes on her tippy toes, and kisses me on the cheek. "I just want to say thank you," she says. "For everything."

I'm taken aback by her sincerity, and before I comprehend what I'm doing, my arms go around her waist in automatic response, and I draw her into a hug.

Her warmth seeps into my damp shirt. I hold her close against my chest. It might be the wrong thing to do, but in the circumstances, it seems so right. She needs someone to hold her and tell her that everything will be okay. And I'm that someone. For a moment, I forget that we barely know each other and that this is just a hug of comfort. A hug between strangers.

"Well, butter my biscuit." Marg's voice rings out, making me do a double-take away from Kat. "I never imagined my little match-making would work so fast."

Kat places a hand to her chest. "Aunt Marg, I didn't know you were a ninja. Scared the living daylights out of me."

Marg wags a finger from side to side, grinning. "What's going on here, hey?"

"Oh." Kat darts a glance my way and back to her aunt. "Clay's offered to be my fake boyfriend until Danny leaves the island."

"Danny's here?" Marg shoots her fists to her sides. "What's he want?"

"Said he wanted to talk."

Marg crosses her arms. "You don't need to give him the time of day. You owe him nothing, Katrina. Nothing."

"I know. I told him so."

Marg drops her arms. "Goodness gracious." She lets out a heavy sigh and shakes her head. But slowly, a smirk appears. "So, you're hugging and practicing your 'fake relationship.'" She uses air quotes.

I bite my bottom lip. What has Kat got herself into? Maybe she shouldn't have told her aunt about me acting as bodyguard. Marg seems quite pleased with herself.

Kat eyes me like she's unsure how I feel about the idea. Am I really going through with this?

I take her hand in mine. "Yep. Gotta be convincing for when Danny sees us together. We can't be all awkward around each other. Needs to look genuine." Inside I'm laughing at my ridiculous excuse to hold Kat's hand. Has my everlasting singleness brought me to this point that I'll grasp at any inkling of a possible relationship?

Kat squeezes my hand and faces her aunt. "Yeah. It's just for a few days. But maybe Danny's left already, and we won't need to worry." She drops my hand, along with my heart.

I was looking forward to playing boyfriend. Wouldn't mind it becoming something real too.

Chapter 6

KAT

Leave it to Aunt Marg to throw an impromptu garden/pool party for all the guests. She sent me a message an hour ago to let me know that things might get loud and I might as well join in the fun.

"All the family will be there." I read her text again and barely resist rolling my eyes. "Nice." It's part guilt trip, part request for me to get out of the unit and enjoy some family time. I can't blame her for wheedling to get me outside. My parents' unit is nice and cozy. I love the beachy atmosphere Mom created with soft blue walls and pastel paintings of sunsets around Nantucket gracing every wall. But it would be nice to get outside and away from the computer.

I thumb back a text that I'm on my way and receive an instant thumbs up emoji in response. Good old Aunt Marg. The woman never can resist sticking her nose in our business. She's been unobtrusive—for the most part—since I came back to Nantucket, but every time I see her, I can sense her need to fix what's gone wrong. She can't help it, and I love that she cares enough to try.

The sounds of the party reach me as soon as I open my door. Splashing and screeching burst through the air like balloons popping in rapid succession. Beneath that, laughter and conversations spill out over the fence.

"Rex, if you dump one more bucket of water on Liam, I'm taking you inside for a nap." Trina's fierce but motherly tone causes my lips to quirk up in a grin.

"No." Rex wails and the sound is followed by another splash.

I don't even try to hide my laughter as I make my way down the sandy path. Roses cover the fence on either side, with the pool's privacy fence keeping everyone hidden from sight.

Nathan walks my way, the path from his house intersecting mine. He's wearing swim shorts and has a towel slung over his shoulder. His eyebrows creep up when he hears the noise. "I'm not sure this is a great idea."

I lift one shoulder and let it fall. "You try telling your mom that we're not coming then." It's easy to goad Nathan nowadays. He's become even more chill since he and Tim finally started working through their problems, but there are a few ways to get him going.

Nathan backpedals so fast his heel catches in a rut and he stumbles into the fence. "And miss out on Dad's grilled shrimp burgers? No way." He shakes his head and grins at the others coming up behind him. Ellie, Preston, Samantha, they're all there. All my cousins and their spouses together create a group that's even larger than the one ringing the pool.

My shoulders tense as I realize I'm the only one walking by myself.

Why does this feel like another setup? Everyone here is married except for me and Clay. I narrow my eyes at Marg when she appears at the gate. Her smile is wide and generous as she holds it open. "Come on. No sense in lurking out here." Bright sunshine bounces off her white straw hat.

We all file in one by one. A lump forms in my throat as I take in all my cousins with their partners. It's a beautiful sight but it also pinches hard around my heart and makes it ache. Why did I marry Danny so fast? I rushed things without thinking them through. Was I so desperate for love that I ignored everything else? I thought I was in love. Danny was sweet and kind. He made me feel special. I'd never encountered anyone like him before. I chew on my lip and pass Aunt Marg.

Her fingers wrap around my arm, the pressure stopping me in my tracks. "Any sign of Danny?"

I bite back the fear clawing up my throat and shake my head. "None."

"Good." She pats my shoulder. "Maybe he's gone back to the mainland. Enjoy yourself, Kat. You've earned it."

Right. Earned it. What does that even mean?

Moving past Aunt Marg, I spot Clay lounging in a chair near the pool. My pulse skips into overdrive and I replay our last encounter minute by minute. Every touch is seared into my mind. What was I thinking agreeing to a fake relationship with him? It's not that I'm intimidated by his good looks. I'm confident in my looks and personality, but there's something about Clay that makes me feel insecure. Maybe it's because he's a doctor. Yeah. That must be it. It's not because he stepped between me and Danny like a knight in shining armor. Or because every time he touches me I feel things that I've never felt before. Things even Danny didn't bring to the surface.

Bless Nantucket and its romantic charm. I'm in a fake relationship with the handsome doctor. Heat blooms in my stomach and spreads outward. He saw me fall apart with Danny and still looked at me with appreciation. I expected scorn or sarcasm after I could barely hold my folder thanks to my shaking hands. How could Danny's presence affect me so severely? It's like no time at all has passed since the last time I saw him in court. He'd been calm that day, but just the night before he'd ranted and raved about how much he loved me. The flipping back and forth wrecked me.

Liam and Adam play a game of water basketball with Rex while Dalton looks on from the side of the pool.

I stop to take in the whole scene and Trina crosses from the side gate to stand beside me. "Is everything okay?"

"Yeah. Fine." I answer automatically to deflect attention and keep from nose-diving into my problems.

Trina follows my line of sight and her lips quirk up in a lightning quick grin. "You and Clay seem to have hit it off."

"He's a great guy." That's easy enough to admit. I dig my sunglasses from my pocket and slide them into place.

Trina focuses on my face, tiny lines fanning out from her eyes when her smile widens. "Yeah, he's something else. I keep hoping he'll find someone to settle down with."

What is it with newly married couples trying to marry everyone around them? They're all happy and in love. Great for them. I really, really need them to leave me out of it.

"Not you too." I groan and turn away, grabbing a bottle of water from the cooler. I'm not meant for love and marriage. Danny ruined that for me. Even if I found someone I could trust, I'd always have that lingering doubt in the back of my mind.

Trina follows when I make my way over to a table and sink into the sun-warmed cushion. "What does that mean?"

I gulp water and then point the bottle at Marg. "Aunt Marg is already trying to set me up with him. After all that with Danny..." I trail off and shudder. "Clay's just being nice. He's pretending so Danny will leave me alone."

A tiny groove appears between Trina's brows. "I think I'm missing something here."

Ugh. Me and my big mouth. She probably didn't know anything about Danny. Which means she didn't know that Clay offered to be my fake boyfriend. If I keep talking, I'm going to make everything worse.

My phone rings and I spot Tim's name on the screen when I retrieve it from my pocket. I grimace an apology at Trina and answer. "Hey, Tim. What's up?"

"Why didn't you call me?" His voice has that gruffness to it that says he's annoyed. "I took a stroll through Danny's socials today. He's on Nantucket."

"Yeah, I know." I rub my forehead with my free hand and stand, mouthing 'sorry' at Trina as I make my way to a secluded corner where I won't be bothered. "He found me."

Tim sucks in a breath and I wait for a blistering string of curses but silence rings in my ears for several heartbeats. "Have you gone to the police for a restraining order?"

"No." My heart races so fast it feels like hummingbird wings in my chest. "I don't have any reason. He just said he wanted to talk."

"Which means he's stalking you," Tim growls. "I swear, Kat." A deep sigh tells me he's worried. "Get a restraining order. You have more than enough reason. I know the law and can assure you that they'll issue the paper without any trouble. You need this."

What good is a piece of paper against Danny? I almost ask, but if I do that, Tim will be on the next ferry to Nantucket. He might be a tough guy who has trouble showing his vulnerabilities, but he is also the guy who shows up when he's needed. Maybe that wasn't always the case, but it is now.

"I'll let Nathan know to keep an eye out." Tim's voice brings me back to myself.

"Aunt Marg already knows. I'm sure she told him." I almost tell him not to bother, but the look in Danny's eyes scared me more than I want to admit. Trusting that he'll stay away is dangerous. I need to be on my guard. "I have someone to be my bodyguard if I go to town." Calling Clay my bodyguard is a bit of a stretch, but telling Tim he's my fake boyfriend is out of the question.

Tim grunts, which is about as close to an agreement as I'm going to get.

"You don't need to get Nathan involved." Sweat gathers between my ear and the phone, making it slick. Gross. I lower my phone and tap the speaker button.

Tim scoffs with enough force to make me wince. "Too late. I've already sent him a text. Do not go anywhere alone." He pauses. "Promise me."

I consider my options. I can promise and mean it, or I can lie. Both have their downsides.

"She promises." Clay's smooth voice rolls out behind me.

"Who's that?" Tim makes a noise that's as close to a growl as I've ever heard. "Kat, answer me."

"That's Clay." I catch Clay's smirk. "He's acting as my bodyguard."

His smile falters a bit at that but he crosses his arms and widens his stance. "No one is going to hurt her. I'll make sure of that."

"I'll make sure of that," Tim says darkly. "Kat, send me his info. I'll run a background check."

I eye Clay and almost take Tim off speaker but it's too late now. "Not happening, Tim. I made a mistake with Danny. I know better than to go down that road again. I don't need you to run a background check." Because I'm not letting Clay get close enough to hurt my heart. I let myself get carried away when I kissed his cheek. That can't happen again. I'll let Clay walk me around town and keep Danny at bay, but that's it. My heart is mine and mine alone. I will not let it get broken again.

"I wish you'd called me." Tim sighs. "I could have been on the next ferry."

My throat burns with emotion that I tamp down before it creeps into my voice. Tim wouldn't appreciate hearing me blubber over how much he's changed this last year. He's always been there for me, even if he fought tooth and nail to keep his brother and his parents at arms length.

"You're right where you need to be," I remind him after I've regained control. "Fighting injustice is what you do, Tim. You're needed on the mainland right now. I'll be fine."

Clay's nostrils flare and his arms flex. Muscle pops out across his torso, reminding me of what hides beneath the baby blue t-shirt. He might be barefoot and dressed for the pool, but one look in those dark eyes and I know that he'd drop everything in an instant to protect me.

It's a weird feeling, knowing that Clay would protect me—a complete stranger. He's a bit more like Tim than I realized. Both have high-profile careers and while Tim fights injustice in the courtroom, Clay hasn't hesitated to put himself in the way of physical harm. Tim would do the same if he was here. Only Tim wouldn't have to pretend to like me.

"Call me if anything changes." Tim's voice turns muffled. "Gotta go. Clay, look out for her or you'll answer to me."

Tim ends the call before Clay can respond. He offers a tiny grin. "I like him."

"Yeah." I clean my phone screen and set it on the table while I drop into a chair. "He has that effect on people. You either love him or hate him." That's not as true as it used to be, but I'm too emotionally drained to delve into the intricacy that is Tim.

Clay takes the seat across from me. Warm hands envelop mine and he rubs his thumbs over my knuckles. "You'll get through this."

I know. I'm made of some pretty tough stuff, even if I did fall apart at the shock of seeing Danny. He surprised me, that's all. I want to say all those things, but the words stick in my throat. Clay's soft touch helps settle me in the moment, and I work to push aside thoughts of Danny and the possible trouble lingering on the other side of the fence surrounding me. "What a mess," I mumble under my breath.

Clay lifts my hands and kisses my inner wrist before pulling me to my feet. "Come on. Let's go have some fun."

Fun. How long has it been since I truly stopped worrying and let myself relax? I'm safe and surrounded by family. There's no way Danny can get to me here.

Grinning despite the nausea curling up the back of my throat as I think about having to walk to town tomorrow, I let Clay lead me to the edge of the pool.

Nathan focuses on his phone, then waves it at me with a stern expression.

Great. Between Aunt Marg and Nathan, they'll all know about Danny by the end of the party. I won't have one person watching my back, I'll have all of them keeping an eye on me. It's touching but also slightly stifling to know that they'll need to know my every move.

Clay steps into the water and lifts his hands toward me. "You coming in like that or is there a bathing suit under there somewhere?"

The words are a challenge and a reminder that I came here to have fun.

Grinning so hard my cheeks hurt, I peel off my oversized shirt and kick my sandals off to the side, then shimmy out of my cutoffs to reveal the black one-piece swimsuit I chose for today. With Clay staring up at me, his mouth hanging open in a state of shock, I slide into the water and plant my hands on top of his head, dunking him before he realizes my intention.

He comes up laughing, and I know right then that I'm in over my head. Because that laugh is one that I'd like to hear every single day for the rest of my life.

Chapter 7

CLAY

The sun glares down on the resort's poolside as I sit on a padded deck chair, the cool breeze offering a momentary reprieve from the summer heat. My laptop rests on my lap, and I squint at the screen, trying to make sense of the jumble of emails that have flooded my inbox. Looks like it's been a busy week at the Oakridge Hospital. Even here on Nantucket, my role as a pediatric surgeon doesn't seem to care about vacation time.

Around me, the clear waters of the pool shimmer invitingly. Families and couples swim and splash about with laughter and playful chatter creating a soothing soundtrack to the day. It's moments like these that make me appreciate the simplicity of life on this island.

A high-pitched voice pierces through my concentration. "Clay, come play with me."

Rex, the Energizer Bunny that he is, hovers by the side of the pool, his arms flailing out of the water for attention. His brilliant blue eyes emanate enthusiasm, and his soaked hair has gone into wild ringlets.

A smile tugs at my lips as I shut my laptop and shove it away from me. Rex is a handful, but he's also totally impossible to turn down. I hurl myself out of my chair and march to the pool's edge, where Rex is practically buzzing.

"All right, buddy," I say with a grin, "what are we playing today?"

Rex's face lights up as he launches into a detailed explanation of the game he's concocted in his five-year-old imagination. I nod along when in reality I have no idea what he's saying. The game seems to involve pirates, treasure maps, and an imaginary sea monster for good measure.

As Rex wraps up his exhilarating explanation, he looks up at me from the pool with an expression that expects my approval. "So, which one do you want to be?"

"Sea monster!" I lift my arms and roar before plunging into the pool.

I'm enveloped in icy-cold water and find his little legs underneath and proceed to tickle his feet. Muffled laughter fills my water-logged ears.

I thrust my body upward, kick to the surface, and flick my hair from my eyes.

He's trying to swim away but his little arms don't give him much speed. Looks like the superpower sunscreen has washed off.

"I'll count to ten," I call across the pool.

Pam laughs from her deck chair. "He's going to need you to count to fifty."

"Looks like it."

Just as I start to forget about work and emails, my iPhone sings out an old ringtone I'd selected—the one that reminds me of my first Nokia.

This snaps me back into reality. I reluctantly freestyle to the edge of the pool, hoist my body out of the water, and check the caller ID, but the call drops off.

I dry my hands and click on the screen again. It's a colleague from the hospital.

I grunt at the inevitable interruption to my vacation.

I return the call, and Theo wastes no time in getting to the point. "Clay, I've been hearing more about the Head of Pediatrics position you're applying for." His voice takes on a serious tone.

I swipe water from my brow and plonk myself on the deckchair. "What's up?"

"Well . . ." Theo sighs. "The board has traditional values. It's composed mostly of older members and they tend to favor applicants who are seen as family-oriented."

I sense where this conversation is heading, and a knot forms in my stomach. "And?"

"And . . ." There's a brief pause. "You're a fantastic surgeon, Clay, but they might not take you seriously because of your age. And you're not married or settled in a stable relationship. The job is demanding, and they prefer someone who has a supportive spouse behind them. Being a family man could significantly boost your chances."

I let out a long breath. "Right. Well, I can't get a spouse overnight, can I?" I huff. "Doesn't this breach some kind of discrimination rule?"

"It's not in writing or a requirement. It's an unsaid thing."

It's frustrating that my qualifications and experience might not be enough to secure a position I've worked so hard for. The reality of navigating hospital politics isn't as straightforward as saving lives in the operating room.

As I end the call and push my phone away, a cloud of doubt hovers over my head.

"Clay!" Rex calls behind me. "Your turn to be the pirate."

I rake a hand through my hair and roll the tension out of my shoulders. I need to be present in this moment and enjoy time away from work.

I return to playing with Rex in the pool, but my thoughts remain tangled in the complexities of work and personal life.

I am a family man. I value my relationship with my parents, my brother . . .

I lift Rex onto my shoulders, his giggles echo through the air.

. . . and this kid—part of my newfound family through Liam's marriage.

Rex momentarily distracts me from the uncertainty that now lingers in the background. Nantucket's serene surroundings offer a temporary escape, but the challenges of the real world are never far away.

KAT

"Grrr." I growl at the computer screen and curl my hands into fists. "Don't do this to me." The black screen flickers and hope flutters briefly in my chest before the laptop makes a whining sound and shuts itself off. The urge to shove it off the table rushes through me and my hands shake as I fight through the surge of anger.

"All I want is to get back to normal." Heat races through my body. I take a deep breath and close my eyes. Getting angry at inanimate objects. Great. Now that's the perfect end to this crappy day. I blow out a tight breath through pressed lips and flex my fingers. I'll try again tomorrow. There are plenty of jobs out there for medical billing and coding in a home setting. I was in the middle of applying to one when the computer went crazy. "Time for a break."

I could use a cold dip in the pool. A swirl of excitement tickles my stomach as I remember dunking Clay during the party. Things kind of spiraled after that. With so many of us around, we ended up playing water ball and Nathan and Preston challenged Clay and Liam to swimming challenges. I think those were more to wear out Rex than anything as the kid tried his hardest to be included in every single game. By the time I went back to my unit, the poor kid was asleep sideways on a lounge chair.

Grinning, I change into a blue swimsuit and sling a towel over my shoulder. Late afternoon sunlight spills across the path and brings new color to the roses. Most of the guests should be on their way to dinner, leaving the pool for me. I'm not in the mood for mindless chatter and noise. I stop at the gate and listen. Silence.

It's easy enough to slip through the gate and lock it behind me, then slip quietly into the empty pool after tossing my towel on a chair. The cool water washes away my annoyance, and I dip under the surface, swimming across the pool length without coming up for air.

Goosebumps pop on my arms when I break the surface.

"Having fun?" A male voice drifts from the table to my right.

I scream and kick off from the wall, sending a wave of water over my shoulders.

"Kat, it's me. Clay." Clay jumps out of the shadows and holds out his hands. "Sorry. I'm so sorry. I thought you saw me when you jumped in. I waved and you looked right at me."

My muscles spasm as the rush of fear ebbs. I gasp for breath and swipe a hand down my face. "I didn't." I still can't catch my breath, so I stop talking and bob in the middle of the pool, kicking my feet to stay afloat.

Clay moves to the edge of the pool and sticks his feet in the water. "Guess we can call that payback for dunking me."

"No way." I shake my head and swim closer. "You took five years off my life. That deserves another dunking."

Before I can react, Clay shucks his shirt and slides into the water without making a splash. Perfect teeth shining, he holds out his arms. "Go on then."

He's messing with me. He has to be. But the look in his eyes says he'll let me dunk him if it'll make me feel better. I cock my head to the side and examine him. "Let's make it interesting. If I can beat you to the other end of the pool, I get to dunk you."

"And if I win?" His smirk widens, crinkling the edges of his eyes and causing butterflies to swarm in my middle.

I smack the top of the water with my palms and push aside the fluttery feeling he's created. "Then you can dunk me. Fair enough?"

He flips onto his back and floats past me. "Let me think about it."

So infuriating. I grab his ankle and jerk him back. "The offer expires in five seconds." I move to the edge of the pool and line myself up for a race. "Four seconds. Three. Two."

"Okay. Okay." He grumbles but is still smiling when he moves into position beside me. "Winner gets to dunk the loser."

"Agreed. First one to touch the opposite side of the pool wins." I settle into position, one hand on the edge and my feet against the wall.

Clay mimics my position. "On my count of three. One. Two. Three."

We kick off at the same time, our bodies slicing through the water with ease. Clay's strong, and his powerful strokes propel him ahead of me in the first few seconds. But I'm no quitter, and being behind doesn't mean I've lost. I cut through the water, using all the skill I've gained in twenty plus years of Nantucket summers and swimming against my cousins. Water sluices over my head when I come up for air and I catch Clay three strokes before we reach the edge. I'm not going to lose. With another surge, I inch past him and slap the wall as his hand comes up from the water.

I give him enough time to take a breath before I put both hands on top of his head and push him under water again.

His arms wind around my waist and he pulls me down with him, dragging water up my nose before I figure out what he's doing.

I slap at his shoulders and push away from him. Bubbles erupt from his mouth and when I look down, he's laughing up at me.

The look in his eyes is too soft, too enticing. I can't trust it. I can't trust him. The knowledge sits heavy as lead. I fight the feeling as I unwrap Clay's arms from my waist and return to the surface. He's right behind me, his presence comforting even as it disorients me. "I have to go." I stomp up the steps as I grab my soft, fluffy towel scrubbing it over my body, then wrap it around my torso.

"Is something wrong?" Clay's quiet question reaches deep and releases the tension coiling through me.

I start to shake my head but stop and turn away. "I just forgot that I need to go to Ellie's." It's a lie. I don't need a thing except to get away from Clay. "I wanted to pick up some muffins for breakfast."

"Kat." Water hits the concrete with a heavy splash, followed by the sound of wet feet slapping. "I'll come with you."

"You do—"

Clay cuts me off with a hand on my arm. "I promised Tim I'd look out for you. You told him I'd go with you if you left the resort." He snatches up his shirt and yanks it over his head as I try not to watch the play of muscle along his back.

Why did I say that? I wasn't thinking straight. Or maybe I thought Clay wouldn't follow through. Either is possible, and both are proving false. Yet more proof that I can't trust myself or my judgment.

He tugs the shirt down and slides his feet into a pair of flip flops. "Okay. Let's go."

"Clay."

"Nope. If you're about to tell me that I don't have to go with you because Ellie's is right down the street, let me save you the trouble." He stops at the gate and holds it open for me. "Do you need to stop at your unit first?"

I'm pretty sure my mouth is hanging open, but I've lost all ability to close it. This guy. Who *is* this guy?

A quick smirk flashes over his face while the fading sunlight brightens his eyes to a deep golden brown. "You're not getting rid of me."

"Fine." I manage to snap my mouth closed and walk past him. I'm not angry, but it helps me focus to stay a step ahead. Clay is the kind of protective that can be appreciated. It doesn't feel oppressive, and I like knowing I can turn my head and see him keeping watch.

I stop at my unit long enough to throw on a shirt and shorts, then we make our way past the resort sign. Downtown Nantucket is in the distance. It's a short walk to Ellie's bakery although once I pass from sandy paths to normal streets, my shoulders hunch forward and my hands curl into fists. I halfway expect Danny to jump out at any moment and make more demands. I won't fall apart this time. I won't let him get to me like that. If only saying it made it true.

Clay moves to my side and slides his hand down my inner arm until our fingers brush. My hand shakes from the pressure of holding it tight and I breathe out a quiet sigh as I unfurl my fingers and Clay twines his hand with mine.

"You're going to be okay." He whispers low but insistent in my ear. "I'm not going to let anything happen to you."

I want to believe him. The fact that I was instantly attracted to him makes me suspicious, though. I trust him enough to walk me to Ellie's and keep me safe from Danny. I don't trust him enough to hand over my heart. I may never trust anyone enough for that.

I drop Clay's hand the minute we make it to Ellie's bakery.

"We're supposed to be dating." Clay grips the door handle and pulls it open for me. "Shouldn't your family think so too? What if Danny talks to one of them and they admit that we're not?"

"They won't." Water drips down my back from my wet hair and the rush of air conditioning when we step into the shop causes a shudder to rattle my spine. "None of them will talk to Danny."

The reminder of our fake relationship freezes my emotions until my entire body feels cold as ice. That's why Clay held my hand and why he's been so attentive. He's pretending.

I'd forgotten about that part of our conversation with Danny. So all of this was for show.

The reminder hurts even as it brings me back to reality.

Chapter 8

CLAY

A knock on the sliding door stops me mid-gulp of downing juice. I swipe my mouth and turn over my shoulder. It's Kat and she's caught me standing at the fridge, guilty of drinking from the carton. The video clip runs in my mind of Liam doing the same thing on *Bride at First Sight*. Although, he had a sticky note stuck to his forehead—one from Trina that said not to drink from the carton.

I should've had the curtains drawn for privacy, knowing that Kat could walk past my glass door and see straight inside. Maybe I have the curtains back for that reason, so I can see when she leaves her unit, and I can coincidentally catch up with her.

I return the carton to the fridge and make my way through the compact living area to meet Kat.

"Morning, neighbor," I say when I open the door.

"Hi..." She uses a gun finger and points at me. "Fake boyfriend."

"Oh, yeah. Nearly forgot." I raise one arm and lean against the door offering a playful grin. "Hi there, babe."

She laughs. "That's not how you talk to a girlfriend in real life, I hope."

I straighten. "Not sure. Most of my adult life I've been studying or working ridiculous hours to get to where I am. Not much time for a girlfriend."

Her lips flatline. "Really? That's sad."

"Tell me about it." I cross my arms. "I only have time for a fake girlfriend. But I intend on changing that." I don't have a plan in place to change my schedule. I've had no reason up till now. Perhaps, the position I'm going for will make it easier to have a meaningful relationship. Head of Pediatrics may or may not be more demanding. More pay, greater expectations most likely.

"I need a favor from my fake boyfriend." She places her hands together in a plea.

"I'm at your beck and call, my lady." I mock bow.

"Ellie needs me for an hour at the bakery. Jarrad's still under the weather, and she has some local deliveries to run. I'll serve at the counter. Can you walk me there and stuff your face with cakes for an hour while you wait for me?"

I tap my chin as if I need to consider such an awesome offer. "You've twisted my arm. I'm in."

"Sweet. Are you free now?"

I glance at the unit which has an empty pizza box on the coffee table, a crumpled towel on the tiles, and one sock beside it. Tidy enough.

"Sure. I'm ready." I grab the key from the wall hook, slip on my flip-flops, and lock up.

We make our way to town, taking the scenic route by the beachside. As we get closer to the main center, my mind races about what I'll do if we bump into Danny. I'm not the get-into-a-fight type of guy. Sure, I work out and I'm bigger than Danny, but if he threw a punch, I might end up with a black eye. That would look great in the interview next week.

"So far, so good," I mumble.

Kat startles and touches her throat. "Sorry, I was lost in thought. What did you say?"

"We haven't seen Danny. Maybe he's not around anymore."

"Oh, he's around. One of my cousins called to say he's still on the island."

"Pity. Means I have to act as your boyfriend a little longer." I take her hand in mine.

She shakes her head, smiling.

We pass a colorful art and crafts store. "There are some quaint little shops in town. I haven't had much of a chance to look through them yet."

"My cousin's wife has her art in that shop."

"Which cousin and how many cousins do you have that live here?"

"Nathan." Kat counts on her fingers. "Ellie and Nathan are Marg and Steve's kids. Tim lives on the mainland. He's Nathan's twin. Then my other aunty has two adult children. My cousin Rachel moved here a while ago. Married the guy who runs the local gym."

"I'm following so far. Barely. Do you have any siblings?"

"One sister, Samantha. She runs Nantucket Adventures."

"Our group is going on one of the yachts this afternoon when the wind picks up."

"You'll have a great time. I'm so proud of my sister. She saved all her money as a teenager and bought her first catamaran. She would rent it out on the weekends during peak season. By the time she was eighteen, she had three mini-cats. Her business grew from there."

"That's admirable."

Amid the hustle and bustle of Nantucket's main street, a colorful spectrum of people surges forward. Couples hold hands as they wander, families with kids in tow gaze wide-eyed at the cute boutiques, and tourists strive to take perfect pictures of the quaint architecture. Locals familiar with the atmosphere of their beloved island, stroll with ease. Except Kat. She's squeezing my hand. Hard.

"There he is." She grabs onto my arm and leans into me.

"Where?"

"Past Ellie's bakery. On a wooden bench seat. He must be waiting for me to visit my cousin."

"That's creepy. He's just waiting there all day on the chance you'll go there."

"He's been on Nantucket with me before. We had breakfast at Ellie's bakery daily, without fail."

Danny is slouched over, clasping his hands, head down. He glances up and down the street, then hangs his head again.

"Phew. He didn't see us." Kat tugs me to the sidewalk and hides us behind a tie-dye T-shirt rack, placing me in front like a shield.

I peer down at her. "He won't make a scene in front of all these people, would he?"

Kat grimaces. "Yes, he would."

"This is ridiculous, Kat. You can't live like this—hiding." I gesture to her cowering low. "He needs to know you've moved on. Completely."

An idea strikes me. "What if we make a scene first? Draw a crowd around us. He won't be able to approach you." And in the process, show Danny that Kat has moved on for good. "Come on." I pull Kat out of hiding and take her into the middle of the street.

She's staring at me like I've lost my mind.

"Trust me." I drop to one knee and look up at her. "Do you think this is a good idea?"

Kat dips her chin and stutters, "Oh my gosh. It's brilliant." A sly smile tugs at her lips. "Yes."

I take a deep breath, sensing the eyes of the curious onlookers. With a theatrical flourish, I throw my arms up in the air and call out to the gathering crowd, "She said, yes!"

A gasp ripples through the spectators, and I spring back to my feet. Kat and I share an impromptu hug, our laughter mingling with the collective tourists and locals.

An elderly lady waves a hand and shouts, "Well, aren't you going to kiss her?"

A teenager calls out, "Yeah. Kiss!"

The crowd's enthusiasm surges and their voices chant in unison, "Kiss her, kiss her!"

I peek over Kat's head, and I spot Danny, a short distance away with his hand shielding his eyes from the sun. This is it. *This is for you, buddy. Back off and leave Kat alone.*

With all eyes on us, Kat and I exchange a conspiratorial glance. She's giving me permission. I lean in and capture her lips with mine.

I planned for a chaste kiss. But as soon as her softness touches my mouth, I surrender my desire to kiss her for real.

People around us erupt in cheers and applause, but the noise drowns away as Kat kisses me back.

Her arms wind around my neck, pulling me closer. My hands grip her waist. I taste the sweetness of her lips, and I want more.

I forget about the onlookers. Forget about Danny. And I forget that we're supposed to be faking this. It's real for me.

But as abruptly as it started, the kiss ends, leaving me reeling, my heart racing. I see the same dazed look in Kat's eyes, and I know that she felt something too.

The circle of people still cheer and we've become the center of attention. We both grin sheepishly. What have we just done? Got engaged—in the middle of Nantucket. Freaking crazy idea, but it's too late now.

We make our way down the street, hand in hand. Danny is nowhere in sight. Whispers and curious glances come from all directions. The warmth of Kat's hand in mine makes me feel a connection that I've not felt before. I know that we're pretending, but something has shifted between us. She's no longer just a girl in need of protection. She's Kat, the woman who has captured my attention and maybe a part of my heart.

I hope to high heaven, we've managed to shake Danny awake. That he no longer "owns" Kat. And he never did. She's not a possession.

Kat halts in front of Ellie's bakery, and spins to face me with wide eyes like what happened has finally struck her. She swallows and blinks. "I live on this island and now everyone thinks we're engaged."

"Ah huh." I grin and lift one shoulder in a shrug. "Hello, fiancée?"

KAT

Steady. My weak knees threaten to collapse at any second. I need to get inside and behind the counter before they give way and send me crashing to the floor. I peer up into Clay's face and try to hide the blush I'm sure has turned my cheeks red. The man can *kiss*.

The fact that it was all part of an act sets my heart back to a sure rhythm. "Ellie's never going to believe this." I wheel around and enter the bakery, where the aromas send a soothing calm over my frazzled nerves.

Clay snorts behind me. His presence is solid and comforting despite knowing that all of this is a ruse to fool Danny into going away.

I nibble my lower lip and hurry toward Ellie. "I'm here."

Her head jerks up and her eyes narrow. "What's wrong?"

"Nothing." I answer too fast, the lie catching me right in the face. Because everything is wrong. I drew the line between me and Clay last night after his reminder that none of this is real. Fake. Fake. Fake. That single word plays on repeat as I school my expression. I fail miserably and finally give up with a huff. "Fine. I'll tell you before Mrs. Potter at the flower shop spills it. Clay proposed and now we're engaged."

Ellie drops the empty plate. It hits the ground and rolls around her feet before bumping against the counter and rattling to a stop. "I'm sorry." Her head shakes side to side in slow motion. She pats her ears and leans in close. "What did you say?"

Should I tell her that it's all fake? What if Danny runs into one of them and pries for information? It's better if they think it's real. At least for now. "You heard me." I round the counter and pick up the plate.

"I couldn't have heard you right." Ellie keeps shaking her head like she's trying to rid herself of a headful of sand. "You're engaged...to

Clay?" She snaps around and peers across the shop where Clay sits at the back of the cafe area with his hands together on top of the table. They're nice hands, I realize. Smooth and capable. And that smile. Swoon. It's probably a good thing he's a pediatric surgeon and not in a position to get hit on by random women. He'd be more popular than that guy everyone calls McDreamy from the hospital show about all the interns.

"Kat," Ellie draws out my name and takes the plate from me. One finger points directly at my face. "We're going to talk about this. As soon as I get back from my deliveries."

Yikes. The stern look on her face holds tightly controlled concern.

I don't blame her. She'll think this is too fast. They all will. It will seem like Danny all over again. It doesn't matter how much they like Clay, they know—and so do I—that I've not spent enough time with him to be in love.

Attracted, sure. But not love.

They're right. I'm not in love with Clay. This is all a sham. A farce. A ploy to get Danny to leave me alone for good.

My chin lifts and I give Ellie a nod. "Later. Go deliver your treats. I'll keep Clay occupied with donuts and coffee."

"Tim's going to blow a fuse," Ellie mutters under her breath.

Cold dread sweeps down my spine. Tim. She's right. My overprotective cousin is going to have something to say about this. A whole lot of something, I'm sure. I should call him and let him in on the secret. Danny won't contact Tim. He knows better, and Tim is likely to hop the next ferry if he thinks I'm about to repeat the same mistake. He's the big brother I never had, and he takes that job seriously.

A middle-aged woman shuffles up to the counter and grins at me. "I just heard the news. Congratulations."

"Thank you." I plaster on the biggest, fakest smile I can dredge up and clasp my hands together beneath my chin. "It was all so sudden.

Such a surprise. He didn't even have time to get me a ring." I raise an eyebrow and meet Clay's eyes over the woman's shoulder. The look is meant to be a challenge, and Clay accepts it with a wink.

We'll sort out our story later. Right now, I have work to do. "What can I get for you, Mrs. Olson?"

The woman taps a finger to her lips and examines the vast array of cookies, hand pies, and pastries. "I'll take one of those pecan cookies." She presses her finger to the glass, leaving a smudge of lipstick behind.

Ellie groans at my back and turns away from the fingerprint. "I'll be back in an hour." The threat remains in her voice. "You better be ready to tell me everything."

I wave her off and focus on picking up the cookie Mrs. Olson pointed out. "There you go. Enjoy."

She pays and carries the cookie to a table right in front of Clay, where she sits facing him and eats the cookie with dainty bites while watching him.

Clay stands and makes his way around the tables. It's mostly empty this time of day, but a few people have wandered in and they keep me busy for the next few minutes. When I take care of the sudden rush of customers, Clay stands in front of me with his hands in his pockets. "How much do you want to tell them?"

I hand him a stack of donuts and slide a cup of black coffee across the counter. "Cream and sugar are on the counter if you want them." When he doesn't move, I blow an errant strand of hair from my face and cross my arms. "I don't know yet. It's all a jumbled up mess in my head." I make a swirling motion around my temple. "Crazy, as Adam would say."

The mention of Adam is supposed to distract him, but Clay's attention remains on me. The singular focus snatches my ability to think and my mind grows fuzzy the longer I stand there with him. None of this is real, I remind myself. He's used to getting what he wants. That has nothing to do with me. Unless...unless he thinks this is some kind of challenge? No. I won't let myself wander down that path.

Clay is good and kind. He's doing this to help me out. There are no ulterior motives.

Chapter 9

It's ridiculous—absolutely bonkers—that I can't have a full week of uninterrupted vacation. Here I am, back on the mainland for an urgent consult. Thankfully, Nantucket is only a quick ferry ride away, but still, this explains why I have no life outside of work. It's all consuming.

My assistant nurse enters the room with a patient and the parent. My heart sinks at the sight of Mrs. Brooks. Dark circles under her eyes show she's sleep deprived worrying about her daughter. I mentally slap myself for complaining about my interrupted vacation. I have nothing worth complaining about in comparison to what parents must go through.

"Here, take a seat." I gesture for Mrs. Brooks to sit opposite me. I smile at the eight-year-old. "Clara, do you want to do some coloring at the craft desk while Mommy and I have a chat?"

Big blue eyes pierce my soul. Trusting. I don't take it lightly that her health is my top priority.

"Yes, please." Clara makes her way to the adjoining room and calls over her shoulder, "Do I get a scratch and sniff sticker if I color within the lines?"

I nod at the nurse. "I'm sure Nurse Anna can make that happen."

"For sure." Anna smiles and passes me the clipboard with the latest test results.

I scan the first page and resist frowning. This is not what I'd hoped for. Surgery is unavoidable now. Making eye contact with the nurse, I flick my head to the doorway. She promptly closes the glass door to the craft room so the child won't overhear the grim conversation I need to have.

I take a deep breath and face Mrs. Brooks. "All the scans confirm my prognosis. Clara has a condition called Inguinal hernia. Part of the intestine protrudes through a weak spot in the abdominal wall. Repair involves surgery to push the intestine back and stitch the abdominal wall closed."

Mrs. Brooks blinks and says nothing.

"The procedure takes forty-five minutes and she'll need two weeks off school. Four to six weeks before returning to any sports activities."

She stutters, "Is there another option?"

I shake my head. "You're welcome to get a second opinion. Our whole team has studied these results. The consensus is that we book her in for surgery ASAP."

She clenches her fists to her chest and after a long pause, nods.

Knots form in my stomach. Being a parent must be a tough gig. I couldn't imagine what it would be like. I would hate for anything bad to happen to Rex and I barely know the kid. He sure has grown on me.

I slip out an information brochure on the condition and go through the details of the surgery with Mrs. Brooks. Ten minutes pass quickly enough and Anna leads them out of the consultation room.

I lean back in my swivel chair and let out a sigh. Glad that's over. I'm better in the operation room than telling parents the risks of surgery. It's never an easy conversation.

Pushing up from my seat, I make my way to my senior manager. It's a good opportunity to pop my head through the door and check in before my interview next week. Show how I'm here when it's needed despite that I'm on vacation break.

The scent of bleach and lemon permeate the white hallways of the Oakridge Children's Hospital. Squeaky rubber shoes echo down the corridors as staff in scrubs pass one way or the other. There's never a moment's rest in this department. Action, go, go, go. Day and night, 24/7. Weirdly, I thrive in this environment.

I push the door labeled, "Head of Pediatrics." The office that I dream will be mine by next month. The position became vacant after Dr. Thomas dropped the bomb that he'd accepted a position in Australia. Can't blame him for taking the opportunity.

Lance grins my way from his seated position. "You can't keep away, can you?"

I shrug and drop into the chair opposite him. "Once I got the email, thought I better deliver the news myself and make sure my patient has the first priority of surgery."

Lance steeples his fingers. "I like your dedication, Clay. But we could've handled this one for you. I can't even remember the last time you had a decent break."

"I've got my eyes on the prize." I point to the open door with the head of department in embossed print. "How are my chances looking? I heard this absurd rumor that the board prefers a family man. That's biased, don't you think?"

Lance raises his palms. "I have no opinion on the matter. But it wouldn't hurt for you to show up to the staff picnic with at least a date, show that you're human and have a social life other than work."

My jaw ticks. "I am human. I just put someone else's needs before mine, five minutes ago. I'm not half a person because I don't have a partner."

"Hey, I hear you." Lance shakes his head. "So no date, no prospects?"

"Man, I don't think you are hearing me at all." My voice is a little more than peeved.

Lance glances over my shoulder and in walks Dr. Russell Gathmore. The surgeon who I have no doubt is applying for the same position as me. The doctor who is married and has adorable twin girls. Blonde ringlets as well. Sickening.

And me? I have no wife. No kids. Not even a goldfish. The last one died after three weeks. Yeah, it's a little sad.

"Russell, will you be coming to next week's picnic? Naomi and the kids coming?" Lance asks.

"Wouldn't miss it." Russell, with his neatly trimmed orange beard, marches to the metal filing cabinet, slips in a manilla folder, retrieves another one, and leaves the office.

I turn to Lance, determination stiffening my spine. "I'll be there too. With my fiancée."

Lance jerks his head back. "You're engaged?"

"Yeah. Proposed on Nantucket. I can't wait for you to meet her. She's the best thing that's happened to me." My throat is drying up with each lying syllable. The proposal part is kind of true. I did get down on one knee.

Who am I kidding?

"Wow. Why didn't you say so? I didn't even know you had a girlfriend. You're full of surprises, Clay."

I stand to my feet. I need to get out of here before the ground opens up and swallows me whole. "Yeah, I surprise myself sometimes." Surprised by how dumb I can be when I have so many letters after my name but lacking a few brain cells when it comes to controlling my big fat mouth.

KAT

I miss Clay. How is it that I can possibly miss a man I've talked to a handful of times? Every time I spot a shadow out my window where I'm working, I jerk around to see if it's Clay coming back from his meeting.

The poor man sat me down like a kid and told me he had to leave Nantucket. He made me promise I'd have Nathan walk me to and from town if I needed to leave the resort. I almost laughed in his face, but the genuine concern I'd seen there stopped me cold and forced me to remember that Danny very well might be a true danger to me.

My palms sweat thinking about it and I swipe them down my shorts while pushing away from the table. I need some air. I've been working all morning and the numbers are starting to blur together. Diagnosis codes flash behind my eyelids every time I blink and I'll likely dream about them tonight. Unless Clay happens to interrupt my dreams again. I'm all for the distraction.

My unit is quiet, just the way I like it when I'm working. Low key classical music plays in the background but otherwise there are no sounds. Sunlight spills across the table and I roll my neck side to side to ease the tension that's gathered there.

Moments like this, I almost wish I had a dog that I could take for a walk. A pet might alleviate some of the monotony from my life and help keep my head on straight when it comes to men.

A shadow sweeps across me where I stand in front of the table. My eyes snap open in time to catch a glimpse of Nathan walking past. He wiggles his fingers at me but keeps going. Probably going to see his mom.

I blow out a breath of disappointment and slide my feet into my flip-flops. I wait until Nathan is around the curve in the path and dart out into the warm light. The salty ocean breeze washes over my tongue and I'm tempted to stand here and bake in the golden glow. But if I do that, Nathan will feel obligated to stay with me if he sees me out here alone. I don't need a babysitter on the resort. I wish I didn't need one in town, but I can't risk Danny getting too close since I never learned self defense. I don't like thinking of myself as helpless, but I'm afraid I would be.

Muttering and scuffling footsteps trickle in from my left. My pulse ratchets up and I press my spine into the warm siding at my back. It takes me a second to recognize Clay's voice and the tension bleeds out of me fast enough to leave me lightheaded.

His muttering continues and he rounds the corner of the unit down from me, his hands shoved deep in his pockets and his head bent forward.

"How was your consult?" I don't know why I interrupt his musing, only that I don't like the way his brow is furrowed or the way he's kicking sand like it personally offended him.

His head snaps up and he stops so fast his body wobbles. "Kat." He looks around, his Adam's apple bobbing. "I didn't expect to run into you."

"You're walking past my unit." I pat the door beside me. "What did you expect?"

"Um." A blush creeps over his cheeks and he palms the back of his neck, then tugs the waist of his pants. He's wearing dress slacks and a pressed white long-sleeve dress shirt with the sleeves rolled up to his elbows. A tie hangs loose around his neck, alongside a pair of shiny black shoes.

"Why are your shoes around your neck?" It's such an odd sight that I can't help asking.

He rocks onto his bare heels. "Didn't want to get sand in them."

"You brought *that* on a vacation." I make a motion with my hand that encompasses his outfit and his blush deepens.

"Well." He stops and straightens his shoulders. "I knew there was a chance they'd call me back to the hospital, so I brought it just in case. I like to be prepared." He said the last bit like it was a challenge.

"Okay. So, how did it go?"

The rigid posture deflates and his shoulders resume their rounded position. His toes dig trenches in the soft sand. "Good. The consult was good."

"Then why do you look like that?" Now, my words challenge him. I want the truth. A man who's come back from a successful meeting doesn't look like that. I should know. I've seen Tim coming back from the courtroom often enough to know what success looks like, and this is not it.

A pair of seagulls squawk overhead and swoop down low to look at us, hoping for a bite of food. I shoo them away while keeping an eye on Clay to make sure they don't make a mess on his nice clothes.

"I've done something you won't like." His voice is low and apologetic.

It snaps me back to those last few months with Danny and my heart stutters. My throat dries out so that I can barely speak, but I manage. "What?"

He winces but meets my gaze. "I'd like you to come to the company picnic as my fiancee."

"What?" My voice screeches so high the gulls answer me and make another lazy sweep. This time, I almost wish they would drop a little surprise. Right on Clay's infuriating head.

He tunnels a hand through his hair. "That came out wrong. Let me explain."

My ears ring, but I listen to his fumbling explanation that he's hoping to be the next head of pediatrics but the men in charge want a family man. Preferably one who's married, but he thought it would be okay since we already had the fake proposal on Nantucket. When he's done, his face is bright red and there's a mix of shame and hope in his steely eyes.

No. No way. "It's one thing to pretend so that Danny will leave me alone." I stumble over my words, a small part of me wishing all this could be real. I squash that thought and dig in my heels. I'm not getting rushed into anything ever again.

"But the whole island thinks we're engaged now." He strides toward me, long legs eating up the distance. "A woman on the ferry asked if we were getting married on Nantucket. She mentioned something about a newspaper."

No. No. No. This can't be happening. "They can print our breakup as easily as they printed our engagement. But what you're asking?" I shake my head because the idea of pretending to be Clay's fiancée is way too appealing. "You're asking me to pretend in front of your entire hospital staff?"

He stops in front of me, blocking the sun.

I need space. Being close to him messes up my brain. I slide to the side and walk toward the beach.

The sound of his steps matches mine as he follows.

I turn and hold up a finger, ready to give him an earful. He's lying. Manipulative. I should have known better. He's as bad as Danny. That last thought is unfair, and it pierces my heart.

A blur of motion pops out from the roses and slams into my lower legs. My arms flail and I lurch forward, straight into Clay's open arms. My chin bounces off his chest and his arms go around my waist.

"Sorry." Rex's voice pipes up as he jumps to his feet and takes off running.

"Please, Kat." Clay's nearness and the way he stares down at me with hope brimming in his eyes is an intoxicating mix.

So intoxicating that I find myself nodding. "Fine. I'll do it."

"Thank you." He kisses my cheek and my bones turn to mush. "Now, we'd better track down Rex. I get the feeling the little guy just pulled an escape."

Laughing, we take off after the boy. Clay catches him around the waist and tucks him under one arm like a football. "Where are you off to?"

Rex kicks. "I wanted to see whales." He kicks again, then gives up when Pam and Dalton rush down the beach. "I'm in trouble."

"Yeah, bud." Clay ruffles Rex's hair. "You sure are."

Chapter 10

I grin wide when Rex's jaw drops as he stumbles into the grand hall of the Nantucket Whaling Museum. Natural light streams through the high windows, illuminating the ivory-colored whale skeleton that suspends from the ceiling like a giant chandelier.

"Holy mackerel!" Rex shouts, tilting his head back to take in the full height of the whale bones. He has never looked so small.

The air in the hall is slightly musty, but a faint scent of saltwater drifts through entrance doors, keeping things fresh. I read the plaque giving some of the history of the area. The rest of our group filter around the exhibition. A long canoe type boat with pairs of oars has grabbed Liam and Trina's attention.

I squeeze Rex's shoulder and point above his head. "The whale skeleton is 46 feet. Pretty impressive, huh?"

Rex only nods, still in awe of the enormous creature before him. He tiptoes underneath its ribcage, looking like he's exploring inside a whale-shaped ship. His fingers stretch high and wriggle to reach a tooth.

An elderly man on guard clears his throat. "You can't touch."

Pam steps beside her son. "Yes, baby. Hands behind your back. Look and no touching."

Rex whips his hands behind his back and pushes out his chest. This kid is adorable.

He turns to me, eyes wide. "Is this really how big whales are?"

"Yup." I ruffle his hair. "Crazy big."

Rex cranes his neck and stares at the skull. Its eye sockets are a little creepy. Despite its intimidating appearance, Rex remains fascinated and pesters me with a barrage of questions as we stroll around the skeleton. "Do whales ever get the hiccups? I bet they're really loud."

Before I can answer, he's onto the next one. "Is it true a whale's pop-off bubble is big enough to fit a car? I want to see that."

"Rex." Pam scolds from behind. "Lower your voice."

I wipe the back of my hand across my mouth, holding back my smile. "Hey buddy, want to ride on my shoulders? You can get a better view."

Rex reverses a few steps then does a run up and climbs my back like a monkey. I help his legs over my shoulders and he slaps his hand to my forehead and pulls himself upright, giving me whiplash.

His Nike shoes dig into my collarbones, but a bubble of laughter makes its way up my throat. Who knew I needed a five-year-old to show me how to lighten up and live in the moment?

Dalton slips his hand into Pams. "Looks like we've found ourselves the perfect babysitter."

"A doctor would do a far better job than Liam and Trina. I wouldn't be worried one bit." Her eyes brighten. "Dalton, we could have a weekend getaway."

I hold up a hand. "Steady on, guys."

Liam punches my arm. "All part of the plan. Trina and I were terrible at babysitting so we wouldn't be asked again. You came to the rescue that night, so 'tag,' you're it."

"He can hear you." I go bug-eyed at Liam, but he just laughs.

As I watch my brother's amusement at my expense, a brilliant idea pops into my head. It might just work. I face Pam. "I can't do a whole weekend, but there's a picnic I'm going to next week. Think Rex would like that?"

Pam blinks as if I'm offering a life supply of chocolate. "Are you sure?"

"Of course. Rex and I had a rocky start, but he's not kicking me in the shins anymore. As long as I listen to his imaginative stories, he seems to respect me when I ask him to settle down."

A deep line forms between Dalton's brows. Doesn't look like he believes me.

I'm sure Rex could behave for one day. I'll show my bosses that I am a family man, and I can handle any kind of challenge. Kat, Miss Rulebook, will be by my side. How hard could it be?

Liam shakes his head. "Wait a minute. You're not talking about the hospital staff picnic. The one where the big guns will be there?"

Rex drums his hands on my head, the rhythm getting faster and harder.

I pat his knee. "Buddy, take it easy up there."

Rex strokes my hair, pushing strands back into place, what feels like a part in the middle.

I wink at Liam. "See, he listens to me."

My brother crosses his arms tight against his chest. "You saw the playback of 'Bride at First Sight'. Rex was literally bouncing off the walls of my apartment. It took the cleaner more than one attempt to clean the scuff marks."

Pam touches her mouth and mumbles, "Yeah. Sorry about that. He does get excited in new surroundings."

"The picnic will be outdoors. Perfect for kids to run around. He'll be charming all the nurses and staff. There'll be other children to play with too."

Trina is giving small shakes to her head. No one seems to think I can handle Rex. Pam and Dalton are willing though. Maybe they're desperate for a break.

"I've got this." I tug on Rex's leg. "Do you want to come to a picnic with me and Kat next week, little man?"

I can't see him but the double kick to my chest as if he's a cowboy tells me Rex wants to go.

"Mom, can I?"

Pam's expression softens. "Sure. You can go with Uncle Clay."

Uncle? I'm not officially an uncle. My brother is. Uncle Clay has a nice ring to it. That would work in my favor if Rex called me "uncle" at the picnic. A real family man. Engaged to Kat and a kid by my side. Hold up. I need to get Kat a ring. Would the board member's wives notice if it's a fake? They'd know a real diamond from a zirconia. Guess I'm going ring shopping. Wonder if Kat will want to come.

Rex bounces on the back of my neck, jarring me out of my thoughts. "Thanks, Mom. I'll be good. I promise."

"There you have it. From the mouth of babes." I wink at Liam.

Trina is biting her lip and Liam drags a hand down his cheek, letting out a breath.

They have no faith in me. Just because they couldn't handle a night with Rex, doesn't mean that I can't be a responsible, fun uncle. I work with kids. This is no sweat off my brow.

I clap my hands together with finality. "It's a done deal. Rex is coming to the picnic and we'll have a blast."

Rex taps my head again, a little too hard for comfort. "Blast! Bang!" He makes some rocket noises.

Liam and Trina collapse into each other, laughing.

I roll my eyes. I'll show them.

Best. Uncle. Ever.

KAT

What have I done? The thought of lying to all of Clay's colleagues sits sour as bile in the back of my throat. Is it too late to back out? Can I shatter the dreams Clay has of becoming the head of pediatrics? I've dealt with enough hospitals to have seen the archaic but unspoken rules firsthand. They're not fair, and that is the only thing keeping me from marching over to confront Clay, telling him the deal's off.

I feel like I owe him for helping me with Danny. The fake proposal was a brilliant move, but now I'm second guessing everything. It's apparently effective, as I've not seen Danny since that day.

Kicking sand, I make my way up the path toward the reception office. I'm supposed to help Marg at the front desk today, but all I really want to do is sit around and consider what I've gotten myself into with Clay.

"I've never seen such a sour face on such a beautiful day." Marg's voice snaps my head up.

She's sitting on the front porch, a glass of ice water in her hand and Steve in the chair beside her. They both watch me, concern pulling their eyes and mouths down in puckered frowns. "What's wrong, Kat?"

Would it be too dramatic to sigh and flop onto the steps like my life is over? Probably. Still, I'm tempted. Instead, I lean against the railing and cross my arms. "I'm supposed to be the person who follows all the rules."

Aunt Marg tips her head to the side. "Is that so?"

"Yes." I drop onto the step and tuck my knees to my chest. With my cheek resting on my knee, I stare up at them. I've always been able to talk to my aunt and uncle. They're like a second set of parents. "I'm good at following the rules. It makes me good at my job. Things make sense that way. Diagnosis codes and test numbers go together. You can't bill an MRI of the head based on a hangnail diagnosis." It's a crude but effective analogy.

"But we're not talking about work, are we?" Uncle Steve gets right to the point. "This have anything to do with that young man? Clay?"

My chest tightens and I tug my knees closer. "I rushed into marriage with Danny without getting to know him first."

"And you're worried the same thing will happen here?" Marg's eyebrows lift and she sips her water. "We heard about your engagement. Anything you'd like to share about that?"

"It's all fake." I close my eyes and give them the details they've missed since my last encounter with Danny. When I'm done, they both wear shocked expressions.

Steve recovers first and moves to sit one step above me. "There's a difference in following the rules and getting in over your head. What happened with you and Danny was not your fault. He intentionally hid part of himself from you. A detrimental part of his personality that you have no control over. That is on Danny. I hope he gets the help he needs to manage his diagnosis."

"And we both hope that you don't allow those few months to distort your entire view on love." Aunt Marg sets her glass aside and leans forward. "You are a bright, beautiful woman. I see why Danny and Clay have fallen for you."

My cheeks heat and I scrub them over my bare knees. "Clay doesn't think about me like that." Our kiss says otherwise, but I can't let myself think about that for too long.

"Oh, we all know that's not true." Marg chuckles to herself but her focus remains on me. "Here's how I see it. You and Clay are both adults. You both know that this 'engagement' is fake." She air quotes engagement but her eyes glitter with delight. "I don't see any rule that you're breaking."

"But we're pretending so that Clay has a better chance of getting the job." I protest.

Marg puckers her lips and makes a raspberry sound. "Bunch of old farts sitting around deciding who's more deserving of a job based on their marriage and not on the person's skills." She waves a hand, batting aside my objection. "Sounds like they need a good wake up call. Or a smack to the back of the head. I never did understand how things like that happened. And in a hospital of all places. That they'd let someone less deserving have a job because they have a family at home..." She trails off, her jaw snapping shut.

"Marg is right." Uncle Steve pats my hands where they hold onto my calves. "I don't approve of lying, even though some people might deserve it. But anyone who looks at you and Clay can see that there are genuine feelings between you."

"I did not need to hear that." Knowing they've likely seen me and Clay walking the beach together, I almost want to ask what they see between us. But I don't need to. I've felt it every time we're together. I'm comfortable with Clay in a way that I was never comfortable with Danny.

"You're on Nantucket, dear." Marg wiggles her eyebrows and fluffs her hair. "Why not let your hair down and live a little. Don't let what happened with Danny ruin the rest of your life."

"It's not like I can forget what happened." An unhealthy surge of anger tightens my hands into fists.

"Of course not." Uncle Steve holds out his hand to Marg, and she slides down to sit beside him, resting her temple on his shoulder. "Learn from your mistakes so you don't repeat them, but don't let them rule you. You have done nothing wrong."

Is that true? I've always felt bad about getting the annulment, even though I know it was for the best. When Danny became irrational and violent, I knew I had to get away from him. There's a small part of me that wonders if I could have helped him. If I'd loved him more, would that have been enough to fix him?

"Stop that." Aunt Marg eases away from Steve and pushes over to my side. Her arms wind around my shoulders and pull me close. "I see those thoughts spinning. You did what you had to do, Kat. Guilt is understandable too, but you are not responsible for Danny's mental health."

I've told myself that same thing time and again, but it feels different coming from Aunt Marg. She tightens her arms and kisses the top of my head. "We love you, kiddo. No matter what decisions you make, you'll always be family. And we stick together."

"Like glue in Ellie's sneakers." Steve grins and the reminder of a prank I once played on Ellie breaks the tension.

I laugh and hug Marg around the waist. "Thanks."

"Anytime." Aunt Marg rocks me side to side. "Now. You pull yourself up out of this glum mood and enjoy some good old Nantucket sun, sand, and water."

The call of the beach is too much to resist. I pull free from her embrace and make my way down to the private beach behind the units. As each step sinks deeper into the sand, I make a promise to myself to stop dwelling on the past and things I can't change and focus on my future. Aunt Marg is right. This place is meant to be enjoyed. It's time I started living my life instead of hiding from it.

Chapter 11

As my time on Nantucket comes to an end, Kat and I must get to know each other more so the board doesn't suspect anything when we meet. She agreed to go on this walk with me.

The wind tousles Kat's hair as we approach the Sconset footpath. She turns toward me, her smile radiant. "I never grow tired of the Bluff walk. I make it a point to come here at least once a week."

Displaying my most charming grin, I reach for her hand. "Lead the way."

She flinches slightly before relaxing and intertwining her fingers with mine.

We pass by some lavish mansions that all seem to have that Old England charm—white framed windows and gray roof tiles. Sprawling lawns and neatly trimmed hedges divide the properties, each with a stunning view of the ocean below.

"So tell me more about yourself," Kat asks. "What's something I should know?"

"My life is pretty boring. I mostly work. Go to the gym. Visit family." I point my finger like a gun when something better pops into my head. "I do play the guitar. Learned when I was a teenager and I pick it up now and then so I don't forget all together."

Kat raises a brow. "Are you any good?"

"I'd like to think I'm good enough. But not that amazing to play in a band in front of a live audience."

"What about an audience of one?" She smirks.

"I can play for you if you'd like. Just need a guitar."

"My uncle has one. Steve used to play too but his acoustic has become part of the decor for the TV room."

"Wish I'd known that before our walk. I could've included it in—" I swallow my words and mumble, "—never mind."

"Never mind what? What are you up to, Clay?" She draws out my name.

My cheeks go flamin hot. "You'll see when we hit the beach."

Kat gets a mischievous glint in her eye. "Fine. Race you to the shore."

I drop her hand and pause my steps. "Thought this was meant to be a nice stroll at a walking pace."

"Not anymore." She grabs my hand and jerks me forward. "Come on."

Before I know it, Kat's got me on an imaginary leash, making me follow like a love-sick pup. We rush past another two mansions before she veers me to a staircase of slate tiles leading to the beach below. My feet jar at the ankles as we pound the steps two at a time.

"Slow down. I'm going to break something," I laugh.

"Nantucket is for adventures, not playing it safe."

"Thought it was for relaxing." My voice tangles with the seabreeze as I follow her.

"You thought wrong."

We weave through scrub and trees making sand kick from our steps. A clearing opens to a crystal view of the Nantucket waves. Kat jerks my arm one more time and I laugh at her bossiness. I like when she's in charge. I like it a lot.

When we're a few yards from the water, she swings to face me, grabs my other hand and pulls me to my knees. She plops into the sand too.

My chest rises and falls as I catch my breath. Kat seems to have an endless supply of oxygen and is able to flash her megawatt smile my way.

"So?" she says.

"Ah, give me a second." Now the time has come, all my thoughtful planning has skipped town. My brain goes blank. How was I going to make this sound logical? Practical?

Kat's gaze never leaves mine. She's waiting for my announcement and soon I'll be waiting for her reaction. Will she freak out?

"Okay." I brush sand from my pants. "I had an idea."

"Yes. Out with it, Clay. I'm in suspense here."

I rub my hands together like it's a fantastic plan. "To make it more believable. Our engagement. I got you a little something." I lean to one side and dig out the jewelry box. I flip it open, and Kat's eyes go wide as moons.

She slaps a hand to her mouth. "Tell me it's fake."

I massage my chin. "I can't tell you that."

Kat tilts her head and leans forward. "Clay! You can't—"

"I already did."

"Will the jeweler take it back after I've used it?"

I shake my head. "Don't think they do that."

"It wouldn't be right to give it to someone else after I've worn it. Won't that be weird?"

"I won't be proposing to anyone else any time soon. You can keep it as a memento. As a thank you for helping me get the position."

"What if you don't get the head of pediatrics?"

I remove the ring from the box and collect Kat's hand. "Don't worry about it. I want you to wear my ring."

Kat frowns. "Are you sure about this?"

Never been so sure about someone in my life. But I can't say that to Kat. She'll bolt and run into the sea.

I offer a reassuring smile. "It would be my pleasure if you'd do me the honor of being my fake fiancée. How about it?"

Kat flips her head back and laughs to the sky. Her giggles carry away in the wind. "This is wild. I can't believe you talked me into this." She flexes her fingers. "Go on. Put it on. Yes, I'll be your fake fiancée."

I slip the ring over her knuckle and like I've seen in a million movies, I instinctively cup the back of her neck and draw her lips to meet mine.

Kat's laughing at first, but her mouth softens and her lips part. It's like the street proposal all over again. Electricity is crackling between us and neither Kat nor I are stopping it.

My other hand threads through her wavy hair and Kat lets out a soft sigh. Her arms go over my shoulders and I close the space between us, drawing in the sweet scent of roses and sunshine. The kiss lasts a few more seconds but Kat must've come to her senses as she pulls back and sits to the side.

She glances to the ocean and back at me. "You're good at the fake kissing thing."

My smile breaks free. "Thanks. Think we can try that at the picnic."

She shoves my shoulder and jumps to her feet. "Try that in public and I'll get Rex to karate chop your knee." Kat laughs and starts running down the beach.

This woman. I'll fall in love with her if I don't be careful. She's everything. Everything I want.

KAT

Pam, Melanie, and Trina stand beside me as we wave goodbye to Clay. My heart does a funny little flip and I miss him even though he's still in sight. This is crazy. Utter madness. I raise my hand and sunlight bounces off the ring he slid onto my finger yesterday. The fluttery feeling escalates until it lodges in my throat. What would it be like to be engaged to Clay for real? I know almost nothing about him, but that hasn't stopped me from feeling insanely attracted to him.

"Ready?" Trina loops her arm around mine and pulls me away from the dock.

I blink away the sudden vision of me and Clay as an official couple and force my lips up into a smile. "Sure." There's a false brightness in my voice that has Trina narrowing her eyes.

"What's wrong?" She leads me toward a series of shops, Mel and Pam hurrying to keep up with Trina's powerful stride.

"Nothing?" I wince when my voice pitches the statement into a question and shake my head. "It's nothing."

"Nuh-uh. You can't get away with that here. Not with me." Trina thumbs her chest. "Sports reporter, remember? I can sniff out a story faster than Rex can eat a whole sleeve of cookies." Which is remarkably fast, as I found out a few days ago when the kid snuck into the kitchen and absconded with his illicit booty.

Pam, Dalton, and Clay had the situation under control in minutes, which was remarkable considering the kid's rather new diabetes diagnosis. He still didn't understand why he couldn't have the cookies.

"Are you worried about Danny?" Melanie asks when Trina stops outside an ice cream shop.

I move off the sidewalk and ease into the shade between two buildings after checking that no one—especially Danny—was lurking in the shadows. "It's nothing." I grin at Trina's raised eyebrows. "Really." I twist the ring around my finger. It feels wrong there, like I haven't earned it. Clay said I could keep it after, but I know I won't. I don't need the reminder of another failed relationship, even though this one is fake.

Pam sets her mom glare loose on me, her folded arms and downturned mouth encouraging me to give in and admit the truth. "You're practically our sister now. You might as well start talking. We can stand here all day."

"Not me." Melanie fans herself with her hand. "I'm roasting. Let's go inside where it's cool. Or head down to the beach."

"If you're worried about Danny, don't be." Trina pins me with her own fierce glare. "He'd be a fool to bother you with the three of us around. We might not have the physical strength, but we make up for it in sheer stubbornness and I for one have no qualms about giving him his marching orders."

The other two women cheer and fist pump the air, drawing attention from a few couples shopping two stores down.

I turn my face away from the curious onlookers and grin. "I appreciate that."

"Do you think he's still on the island?" Melanie takes a paper fan from her back pocket and waves it in front of her face. Her flushed cheeks encourage me to lead them down the sidewalk toward Ellie's bakery. I wait until we're out of earshot before I answer. "I haven't seen any sign of him. Even Nathan and Preston say he must have left after Clay's proposal." I spin the ring again, my hands tucked in tight to my stomach. I admitted to Marg that the whole thing is a farce, and she helped me tell the rest of my family. I'm not sure if I should admit the truth to Pam and the others. They've treated me like family, and part of me doesn't want to ruin that. But the dishonesty sits heavy in my stomach.

Pam pulls the door open at Ellie's and ushers us inside. The delicious smells crash over me and my defenses lower. I'm safe here. Even if Danny sought me out at the bakery, there are too many people around for him to get close. I want this nightmare over once and for all. What will it take to convince Danny to leave me alone for good?

"I'm worried for you." Trina says it in that no-nonsense way of hers.

Of all the things I expected her to say, that wasn't one of them. "Why?" Does she think I'll be disappointed in my marriage to Clay? As far as they're concerned, this is the real deal. I have to tell them the truth.

"Without Clay here, Danny might think he can try again." Melanie grabs a seat at the empty table in the back. The same one Clay sat in the last time I helped Ellie.

Why does everything remind me of Clay? This is Nantucket, my home away from home. It has tons of good memories for me, and they're being tainted by Danny's foul temper and now my feelings for Clay. "I'll be fine." I try to shrug but the movement is stiff and unnatural.

Trina catches it and her frown deepens. "You should go to the police. Get a restraining order."

A sigh presses against my sternum. "Why does everyone keep saying that?" I hold up a hand to stop them and continue. "It's a good idea, in theory. When have you ever known a piece of paper to stop a man like Danny? If anything, knowing I've gone and done that will enrage him even more." A glancing pain thrums in my temples.

Ellie spots us from behind the counter and rushes to plate up a stack of treats, along with coffees.

I should go help her, but it all weighs on me so much that my feet are stuck to the floor.

"You're not listening to yourself." Trina plants her palms on the table and leans toward me. "If you get the restraining order and Danny violates it, he'll go to jail. Then you'll be safe and there's a good chance he'll be forced into getting help for his mental state."

The idea intrigues me...until I remember the look in Danny's eyes when he confronted me and Clay. A shudder wracks my spine. "I doubt Danny is even on the island anymore. A restraining order isn't necessary."

"Denial." Pam's voice is so quiet I almost miss it. "You're burying your head in the sand, Kat. That's not healthy."

"Yeah, well." I grab a cookie from the platter as Ellie sets it on the table. "Neither is faking an engagement with Clay so Danny will leave me alone and Clay has a better chance of getting the job he wants."

Stunned silence greets my outburst. The delicious cookie turns bitter and dry in my mouth. I take several gulps of coffee to wash it down and rub my eyes. "I'm sorry. I didn't mean to tell you like that. It's just. You've all been so nice, and I don't deserve it. This whole thing is fake." I tug on the ring, ready to rip it off my finger and throw it.

Mel grabs my hand and wraps it in both of hers. "Don't do that. Don't push us away. It doesn't matter. We all see that you and Clay have feelings for each other." She grins at Ellie. "And as someone who once threw my wedding ring away in this very bakery, I don't recommend it."

A laugh bursts out of me and I sink into the chair, all the fight draining away. Everyone knows now. Everyone but Danny and the people Clay hopes to impress.

Worry nibbles at me. How am I going to convince a hospital board that Clay and I are the real deal? My tendency to want to avoid trouble makes it difficult enough without adding the extra strain of a fake relationship to the mix. I can't even bring myself to face Danny or get a restraining order. A groan works its way up my throat. The picnic is going to be a disaster.

Chapter 12

CLAY

"Big smiles, everyone," I say through gritted teeth as I make my way across the grass, Kat and Rex in tow. Kat gives my arm a pinch while no one is looking, likely payback for getting her wrapped up in this charade as my fake fiancée for the hospital's staff picnic. But I need this promotion and the board is here, so it's showtime.

I wave enthusiastically to the directors gathered around the picnic tables, leading Kat and Rex right up to them. "Lovely day for a staff bonding event, don't you think?" Man, I sound cheesy. I'm not good at this.

I put my arm around Kat's waist, getting a slight elbow in my ribs when I pull her too close. But she's a good sport and plasters on a smile as I say, "I'd like you to meet my beautiful fiancée, Kat, and my amazing nephew Rex."

At this, Rex becomes shy for a moment and grabs onto Kat's skirt, hiding half his face. I haven't seen this side of him before. That would be a bonus if he stayed quiet for the entire day. Here's wishful thinking.

"What a pleasure to meet you both," Ms. Pembroke, the chairwoman of the board chirps in an overly enthusiastic tone. "Clay keeps his personal life private so we didn't even know he had a family on the way."

Kat touches her belly and eyes me cautiously. "Clay, sweetheart. What have you been announcing without my knowledge?" She mutters under her breath but loud enough that Ms. Pembroke frowns.

I squeeze Kat's hand. "Nothing, darling. Honey bun." I smile confidently at Ms. Pembroke and Dr. Arnold who joined us. "We're not rushing an engagement because of any reason other than we felt it was right. We are getting older and yes, it would be nice to start a family, but we're enjoying being uncle and aunt to Rex for now."

Kat's shoulders lower and her smile returns. "Yep, we adore spending time with Rex." She pinches his cheek for effect.

He wriggles out from behind her skirt and yells, "Ouch! Don't. Do. That."

A trickle of nervous sweat dribbles down my back. This is not the start I was after. What's with all the pinching, Kat? Sure, Rex has cute, chubby cheeks, but she hardly knows him enough to know how he'd react. I barely know him. We're doing a terrible job of acting as uncle and aunt. Three minutes in and we suck, big time.

"Sorry, I didn't mean to—" Kat begins but it's too late. Rex takes off running.

"Buddy," I call. "Kat was just—" I turn to the board members. "Be right back." I take off after Rex. He's heading for the playground. Hopefully Kat will cover our blunder and charm the directors while I'm gone. I have the more difficult task of winning over a five-year-old.

The kid is quick.

I catch up to Rex as he reaches the top of the slide. He flashes me a mischievous grin. He's not upset. He's playing me. "Come and get me," he challenges.

I chuckle at his antics, and climb the ladder after him, ready to fully embrace the fun uncle persona.

Halfway, I glance over to Kat and the others. Lance and Anna are there too. They're standing in a semi-circle watching us. This is my moment. Show that I'm not all about work and know how to have fun, living a balanced life.

Rex launches himself down the twisting slide, and now it's my turn.

I plop down at the top, my long legs bent to my ears. Wriggling to get comfortable, I acknowledge I've underestimated the squeeze factor here. Plastic edges dig into my sides as I slowly scootch downward like a worm.

My slacks inch higher and higher, and my underpants give me a wedgie. I wave nonchalantly to Kat like I'm having the time of my life. The slide narrows even more halfway down and my torso won't fit. I strain, sucking in my gut desperately but that somehow jams me in tighter. I'm . . . I'm stuck.

Rex is below, shielding his eyes from the sun. "What's taking so long?"

"Uh, a little help here?" I call in a casual voice. Inside I cringe as other kids Rex's age point and openly laugh.

Even from afar, I notice Kat covering her mouth behind a polite hand. Wonderful. Of all the ways to impress the board. Will I need Nurse Anna to dislodge me from a tiny slide?

"Looks like you're stuck, Uncle Clay." Rex's grin grows wider as he watches me struggle.

"Help a guy out and give me a push from behind?" My voice sounds uncertain even to my own ears.

In a flash, the kid is up the ladder.

I peek over my shoulder. "A gentle shove in the back should do it."

Rex positions himself in a horse position, gets a good grip on the metal bars, and then . . . bucks with all his might, slamming his feet into my back.

All of the air is knocked out of me.

He does it again.

And again.

"Dude." I manage to hold up a hand. "I mean, kid, that's enough help, thank you."

Such a bad idea. I heard Liam call him Wrecking Ball Rex one time. Now I understand. I feel like a wrecking ball swung into my back three times over.

I need a new strategy. And quick.

I grab the material of my slacks from one side and thrust my thigh sideways.

It works, but my elbow cracks into the slide. "Argh! Funny bone. Not funny," I whimper.

"Are you okay?" Rex's cute voice asks from behind me. He actually sounds concerned this time.

"No. Not okay." I double over into the fetal position and rub my elbow. "Flipping heck that hurt." I peek up at Rex and hope he didn't hear me. He better not go back home to Pam and repeat Uncle Clay's phrases. I'll get the sack and be demoted to Liam's brother.

KAT

I smother a laugh behind my hand and focus on the man standing beside me. Clay didn't offer their names, but I've been around hospital types often enough that I don't think it will be a problem. Rex continues to try and help Clay out of the slide. The howls from Clay mix with Rex's laughter and I almost lose my ability to appear nonchalant. I should probably be more concerned, but it's too funny.

Grinning, I wave a hand toward the playset. "It's wonderful to see them enjoying themselves."

The older man nods, his mouth furrowed in a tiny smirk. "Yes. It's...something."

I swear he snorts out a laugh but is too polite to really let loose.

"He loves Rex." I'm playing it up a little too much, but I might as well go all in. "We both do. He's a handful, but we don't mind a challenge." There. Let them read whatever they want into that.

"Clay certainly is a team player." The man looks at the woman and smiles down at her.

A pair of familiar faces appear to my right. I gasp and clasp a hand over my mouth. "Tim? Kayla?" I wave until I gain Tim's attention.

His brow furrows and he cups Kayla's elbow while leaning down to speak into her ear. They both turn and head my way. Kayla keeps pace beside Tim's long strides, and my heart warms to see him up and walking with ease.

"What are you doing here?" Tim gives me a quick hug, but his body is tense, almost like he's uncomfortable.

"Tim." Kayla elbows him and shakes her head with a look of consternation. "Excuse him. He's in a mood."

"It's not my fault." His scowl eases a bit when Kayla rolls her eyes. He chuckles beneath his breath and takes Kayla's hand. "Okay. Okay. I'm being a bear."

"I told you that you didn't have to come." Kayla leans in close and whisper-shouts. "He's antsy because no one here speaks his language and he doesn't want to spend all day talking about every doctor's worst day in surgery."

"I've been told four horror stories so far." Tim holds up four fingers and shakes his head. "Four. At this rate, I feel lucky to be alive but I'm concerned about anyone who goes to their hospital."

"The statistics for doctor related deaths in surgery are quite low." The man Clay left me with interrupts our conversation with a pleasant tone, but there's a lingering note of steel in his eyes. "Oakridge is one of the best hospitals in the states."

"Uh-huh." That spark I know so well appears in Tim's eyes. My cousin loves to argue. He lives for it, which is part of what makes him a great lawyer. "One of the best, but not *the* best. What would it take to put you at number one?"

The man splutters a bit.

Clay's bellow of irritation causes my stomach to knot. I turn around and face the slide in time for Clay's feet to hit the ground. He stands and straightens his shirt and tie, his face flushed bright red. He swings Rex off the slide as he zooms down, catching him before Rex knocks his legs out from under him.

"Again." Rex bounces and laughs a big belly laugh that even Clay can't resist.

Clay lowers Rex to the ground before his flailing feet leave bruises.

I can't hear their conversation, but after a bit of chatter back and forth, Rex takes Clay's hand and walks back over to where we stand.

Tim's head jerks around and he gives Clay a long look.

"Tim, this is Clay." I almost say 'my fiancé' but bit it back at the last second while hiding my ring hand behind my back.

Clay doesn't miss a beat but sticks out his hand. "Pleasure to meet you in person. I didn't expect to run into Kat's cousin today." He's open and curious as he stares at Tim. "You look just li—"

"Don't say it." Tim holds up a hand. "Nathan and I are twins. But that doesn't mean we're anything alike."

Kayla makes a little noise in the back of her throat and wraps her arms around Tim's waist. He moves an arm over her shoulders in such a natural reaction that it makes my heart ache for what I'm missing.

I try to avoid the feeling, but it roars up every time I look at Clay.

Clay's smile stretches wide. "I was going to say that one movie star from *Hero Rock*. But yeah, now that you mention it, I see the resemblance to Nathan."

Tim's shocked laugh bursts out. The sound is so foreign and unexpected that I gape at him. Clay did that? Clay made the sulky and perpetually dour Tim *laugh*?

"That's a good one." Tim shakes a finger at Clay. "How are things on Nantucket?" He eyes me and all the laughter dies in an instant.

Clay's doctor friends have wandered off to join more of their colleagues. I'm grateful for the reprieve but also anxious to have this day over with. The large field spread out all around is vibrant with freshly mown grass that tinges the air and lulls me into a false sense of security.

"No sign of Danny." Clay slides his hand down his tie and straightens it again. The nervous energy radiating off him surprises me. Is he nervous because of Tim or that he's not made the best impression on his colleagues?

A group of children run past us. One taps another on the shoulder. "Tag. You're it."

"No fair," the boy shouts back. "You didn't wait long enough to start running."

"Clay?" Rex pulls on Clay's waist. "Can I play?"

"Not now." Clay motions at all the staff moving toward the side of the field. "We should join them."

Tim's gaze lands on me and I do my best not to fidget under his heavy look. There's a reason he's called a shark in the courtroom. One drop of nervous energy and he'll be all over me with a million questions. He takes his time but eventually allows Kayla to pull him into motion. "What made you decide to come to this thing?" Tim waves one hand in a careless shrug. "Never known you to bother with social gatherings. You working for this hospital now?"

Caught. I'm stuck in the web of lies Clay and I created. If I tell Tim about the fake engagement, he's as likely to storm off and confront Clay as he is to take it in stride and let it go. He's overprotective to the point of annoying, but I love him anyway. "I came with Clay. I'm not working with the hospital, but I thought it would be a good opportunity to meet some new people. Maybe they can send some work my way."

I talk too fast, the words tumbling over each other faster and faster until I'm out of breath.

Rex bounces up and down. "This is boring. I want to go play. Is there going to be food? I'm supposed to eat cuz of my d'betes."

Kayla's brows arch.

"Diabetes," I clarify. Pam gave us a whole list of instructions. Things Rex could and could not eat. Thankfully I have some knowledge of the situation after years of billing and coding, and Clay is a doctor. Rex is in good hands. As long as we can keep him in sight and out of trouble.

We join the fringes and Clay lifts Rex onto his shoulders. "We'll get you some food, little man. Don't you worry about that."

No. We have much bigger problems. Like getting out of here without everyone finding out this whole thing is a setup to make Clay look good. Sweat slicks my armpits and I've never been more grateful for strong deodorant and capped sleeves and I repress the sudden shudder twitching my shoulders. I wish I'd never agreed to this, but I owed Clay. And I can't say I regret the time we spent together on the ferry, then the drive to the park. Even Rex's constant chatter didn't dull the pulses of attraction between us.

Chapter 13

CLAY

Tim scans my whole body like an MRI machine making me feel stiff and claustrophobic despite that we're in open air and sunshine. Is this how he wins court cases by making the witness confess every detail?

I don't have time for chit chat with Kat's cousin. We have a mission today and that's to impress the big guns before my interview. I shake out my arm and face Kat. "I need to spend more time with the board. Are you okay if I leave Rex with you or are you able to join me?"

"Isn't this a casual picnic?" Tim slips a hand into his jeans' pocket. "What's the urgency?"

Kayla rolls her eyes. Looks like Tim has the same problem as me. Doesn't know how to quit work and relax. This guy has me on the witness stand and I haven't committed a crime.

"I have a job interview next week for head of department. They prefer someone who's family oriented, so that's why I brought Rex and Kat."

Tim shakes his head and frowns. "Kat's not your family. I'm certainly not related to you."

At first, I liked Tim, but he's becoming as annoying as a mosquito when you're desperately trying to sleep. You want to find that bug and squish it into silence.

"Kat's helping me out. I told Danny we were together to get him to buzz off. Now she's returning the favor and acting as my fiancée."

"Hold on." Tim snaps his head to Kat and back to me. "You're lying to your bosses to get a promotion? That doesn't sound integral." He frowns at Kat. "And you agreed to this?"

Kayla loops her arm around Tim's and rubs his bicep. "Hon," she whispers.

He briefly kisses her cheek and returns his laser glare onto his cousin. "So?"

Kat shrugs. "I don't have a problem with it. Why should the board have a prejudice against Clay because he's a hard-working bachelor? He deserves the position and it's ridiculous that they have this stupid rule about him needing to be in a steady relationship."

Tim unloops his arm from Kayla's grip and straightens. "There's no rule. That would be illegal."

"It's not a requirement," I interrupt. "It's an unsaid bias. The board is made up of seniors and they firmly believe that men work better under stressful demands if they have a supportive family behind them. Family life keeps them balanced."

"I admit that coming home to Kayla helps me destress from a hectic day. I see their point. But it's still workplace discrimination. You should apply for the position on your own merits and if you miss out to another applicant based on relationship status, they could face a lawsuit for breaching Equal Employment Opportunity."

I hold up a hand. "I'm not going to stir trouble. I have a great working relationship with these people, and I love the hospital I'm at. I don't want to ruin a good thing."

"It's fine, Tim," Kat says firmly. "Look, we need to go. Nice seeing you both." She smiles at Kayla but ignores her cousin.

Relief washes over me until I dip my chin to find Rex digging holes in the grass with a stick and dirt is smeared all over his shirt. "Buddy, let's get you some lunch. First, we need to wash those hands of yours."

He squints up at me. "About time." He jumps to his feet and brushes his hands. "Adults talk too much."

Hopefully he doesn't say smart remarks like that to the board. We say our goodbyes to Tim and Kayla, get Rex washed up, and remove as much dirt as we can before returning to the spread of food set out on the wooden table.

The picnic table barely has any space remaining. Only a glimpse of the checkered tablecloth can be seen. In the center sits a country-style potato salad loaded with hard-boiled eggs, celery, onions, and a creamy dressing. Next to it there's a vibrant orange and red pasta salad packed with chopped vegetables.

Several platter baskets overflow with fried chicken, the crispy skin making my mouth water. But my stomach growls at the stacks of turkey and ham sandwiches on artisan breads. Bowls are mounded with fresh watermelon triangles, strawberries, grapes, and pineapple chunks.

Were we meant to bring something to contribute? Crap, I think there was an email about that. That's a missed opportunity for me to show my domestication. Or have Kat show off a signature dish like the supportive yet-to-be spouse.

I grip Rex's hand tighter and pull him to my side. "Wait up. We need to test you first."

He groans loud enough to get some attention from Anna. "I feel fine."

Kat brushes his hair from his eyes. "And we want to keep it that way."

Nurse Anna makes her way over and kneels beside Rex. "Hey there. Looks like you were having so much fun with Uncle Clay on that slide. You were super helpful." She smiles up at me and winks before focusing on Rex. "Can I help you with your prick test? I'm a nurse."

"And it's your day off," I say.

Anna squints at me. "And you can sure talk about days off, Doctor Clay Ashley."

Rex nods at Anna. "Do I get a jellybean after?"

"We'll see." Anna takes him to some nearby shade and attends to Rex.

I hand Kat a paper plate and grab one for myself. "Let's eat."

Twenty minutes pass and Rex is off playing with other children on a seesaw. So far so good. I lead Kat to one of the board members who's finally finished talking to my rival for the position, Dr. Russell Gathmore. His twin girls wear matching dresses and pigtails today. Talk about soft sell marketing.

"Tony," I say as I slide up next to him, Kat's fingers entwined with mine. "What a splendid day it turned out to be."

Tony's brow twitches. "Indeed." He smiles at Kat. "And this is?"

"My fiancée, Kat. She works in the industry too."

Tony nods. "What do you do, Kat?"

"Administration for medical firms. Billing, reports, data entry." She rattles off more detail and Tony seems impressed by her knowledge. I'm impressed too. It didn't click before how much she understood about medical systems.

Tony taps a finger to his chin. "I have someone who might want to use your services. Are you taking on any other clients?"

"I do have room for another. Depends on the job."

"I'm having dinner with them next week. Would you and Clay like to join us? I could introduce you."

She turns to me. "Will you be working in the evenings?"

This is a perfect turn of events. If it's before Friday's interview, I'll get to spend more social time with Tony. I smile in his direction. "What day?"

"Tuesday."

"Perfect." I rub Kat's hand. "We'll be there."

KAT

What a day. A deep exhaustion has me blinking back yawns as dusk settles around us. Rex is curled up against Clay's side, his little knees drawn up to his chest. A soft snore flutters his lips and mine quirk in a quick smile. "I think we wore him out."

Clay glances down and his face softens. "I'm terrified that I'll wake him if I move." He reaches for my hand and laces our fingers together. "Today was a good day."

"It was. Is it weird that I'm low key excited about that dinner next week? I know it's more about you getting the head of peds job, but a new client, and one so well connected, could be a game changer for me."

"They were impressed with you." He kisses the back of my hand. "I was too." A beat of silence passes before he continues. "Thank you for doing this. I'm glad you'll get something out of it too."

My stomach clenches at the reminder that all this is fake. It's like we're bartering services or something. I go on a dinner date with Clay and we both get new jobs from the deal. Tim's words come back to haunt me. He's right. The hospital can't deny Clay the job just because he's single.

But just like I won't rock the boat and take out a restraining order on Danny, Clay doesn't want to risk upsetting the entire hospital's upper staff by claiming discrimination. Even if both are valid.

"Are you sure you don't mind taking Rex back by yourself?" Clay's thumb glides over the back of my knuckles.

Eying Rex, I pretend to consider the question until the silence stretches into something uncomfortable. Finally, I grin. "It's fine. If you take the ferry back to Nantucket, you'll be stuck until morning since this is the last one of the day. You need to be here for your big interview." I remember Rex's reaction to my cheek pinching and grimace a little. "He likes me now, and I think he's too sleepy to be much trouble."

"Don't count on it." Clay lifts his free hand to the side of my face and brushes a strand of hair away from my cheek. "I'm going to miss you."

My heart somersaults, and my pulse races. This is not good. I can't have real feelings for Clay when our entire relationship is based on lies. "You can stop acting, Clay. No one is here to see." I need him to go back to the cool and aloof Clay I first met. This tender and sensitive version has my emotions sparking all over the place.

"Who says I'm acting?" He whispers it so low I almost miss the words, but when he leans toward me, I can't resist closing my eyes.

Warm lips brush over mine in a featherlight kiss that's so soft I barely feel it. I expect him to pull away, but he returns, his lips capturing mine as his hand slides to the back of my head.

I'm lost in the sensation of Clay's lips and his embrace. Our engagement might be fake, but this, this is real. I lose track of time. Nothing matters except the feel of Clay's lips and the slow fire building in my veins. I've never felt anything like this before. It should scare me that I can't seem to tear myself away from Clay. I lean into his touch and grasp his shoulder to steady myself before I slide right off the bench seat.

A cool mist stirs from the water beneath our feet, the dock swaying gently. Or maybe that's my body. I can't tell anymore.

A blast from the ferry horn startles me so bad I wrench away from Clay. My head knocks into the light post behind me and stars flash behind my eyes. "Ouch." I rub the tender spot and scowl at the ferry pulling up to the dock.

Clay appears dazed, his entire face is slack, his mouth hanging open the slightest bit. He snaps it closed and runs a hand through his hair. The strands stand on end and I fight the urge to smooth them back down.

Rex bounds to his feet. "Whoa. That scared me. Why'd they do that? Are they gonna crash?" He cups his hands around his eyes like binoculars and leans forward.

"They're not going to crash." I reassure him quickly before he can come up with a million bad things that might happen while we're on the ferry. The last thing I need is for Rex to go home and tell his parents that we almost died in a ferry crash. The kid has an imagination unlike anything I've ever seen. I hold out my hand to him. "Are you ready to go home?"

Rex peers at me through his binocular hands. "I can't wait to tell Mom about the picnic." He swivels to face Clay. "You were funny on the slide."

Clay rubs his hip and winces. "I'll have bruises for a week. But I'm glad you had fun." He holds out a fist, and Rex bumps his tiny fist against Clay's larger one.

Rex lets me take his hand and we turn away. Why does it feel like I'm leaving my heart behind with Clay? It's a fanciful notion and I do my best to ignore the thought. Rex bounces beside me, peering around like he's never been on the ferry before.

"Kat?" Clay calls out behind me.

I turn and find him standing beneath the street light. The dull glow creates shadows beneath his eyes and shows off his sleek dress pants and white shirt.

He shoves his hands deep into his pockets. "I'll call you, okay?"

"Okay." Because what else can I say? We have no further obligation to each other. While this feels real, that will fade once I'm back on Nantucket and he's running the pediatric department. We've gone from friends to fake engagement, to...whatever this is. Uncomfortable strangers who just kissed.

Rex tugs on my hand and strains toward the ferry. "Can we stand at the top? I want to see 'tucket. I bet we can see the whole world from up there."

Clay and I end things like a couple of teenagers uncertain of the next step. The ubiquitous "call you later" implies that I will in fact not hear from Clay at all. It's like the "we need to talk" situation. Sheesh. It's funny how words have certain meanings that we ascribe to them whether the speaker intends them that way or not. I try to keep my head clear of reading too much into Clay's words. The way he kissed me says he feels something too.

"Come on, Rex. Let's see if we can find a spot." I force my lips into a smile. My dress catches the breeze and billows around my legs. I gather it in one hand. Thank goodness I had the good sense to wear flats today instead of heels. It makes traversing the dock and the ferry deck much easier as Rex and I wind our way around the lower deck and up the stairs. The upper deck is completely empty. I lead Rex to the rail where he'll have a perfect view of the ocean and Nantucket.

It's time I stopped living in the fairy tale and came back to reality.

Chapter 14

KAT

It's been two days since I left Clay standing on the dock while Rex and I returned to Nantucket. Two days without a word. I scowl at my phone, then huff and push it across the table. "Get hold of yourself." I expected this. He didn't say *when* he'd call. For all I know, he might wait until he's on his way to pick me up Tuesday for our dinner date. Wait. Is he picking me up or am I supposed to meet him on the mainland? We never clarified. Dang it. I chew my lip and consider calling him. My fingers twitch toward my phone, but I snatch them back and curl them around my mug of tea. I'm not going to be that person who sits around waiting for him to call.

I want to be. As desperate and pathetic as that sounds, I want Clay to be the one to make the next move.

"You're being ridiculous. Call him and tell him how you feel." I sip my lukewarm tea and splutter at the bitterness. "Great. I forgot the honey." I smack a palm to my forehead. "And I'm talking to myself."

Tim would say I'm seeking expert advice. His familiar smirk flashes in my mind as I roll my eyes even though there's no one there to see. I need to get outside. The walls feel like they're closing in around me. Even the air is thick and heavy despite the air conditioning.

Standing, I head to the sink and dump the tea down the drain then rinse my cup and set it aside for later.

Regret slices through me with the swiftness of a scalpel. I never should have let Clay kiss me. We took things too far when there was no need. That's the reason my stomach is tied up in knots and Clay is all I can think about. I stomp to the front door, grab my sunglasses from the tray, and slide my feet into my pink flip-flops. I need the ocean with its shushing waves and the brightness of sunshine on my face. Light hits me as soon as the door opens until my sunglasses are in place, and I blink to clear my vision.

Childish laughter rings out from the pool area, and I almost turn that way. I could use a bit of laughter and distraction to keep me from accepting the truth. I need to end things with Clay. Like officially end them. The fake relationship and all that goes with it. There's no need to keep it going.

"Morning, Kat." Aunt Marg greets me from down the path with a smile that drops when she takes a look at me. "Where's the fire?"

"Nothing. I mean, nowhere." I bite down on the urge to blurt out everything that happened over the weekend. "I'm headed down to the beach." I wave in that general direction.

"If you're not busy this afternoon, I could use some help in the office." Aunt Marg tips her head to the side and it's like she looks right into the part of me that's hurting. "I'm having a big dinner for Liam and the others. You should join us."

She's mentioned a few times that she doesn't think it's good for me to sit in my unit alone all day. It's okay when I'm working, because I like the quiet, but times like now, my mind spins and spins until all my thoughts turn upside down. "Thanks. I'll try to make it." I give her a quick hug before I turn and jog toward the waves. I don't stop even as I kick off my flip-flops until I'm ankle deep in the water. Each retreating wave sucks sand from beneath my feet, forcing me to constantly shift my weight to keep my balance.

The horizon stretches out in a straight, unbroken line. No ships dot the expanse of blue today. A storm brews, gray clouds stretching low and dark. They're too far out to be a bother to us, but the sight of them wrenches deep within my heart. That's all Clay and I are to each other, a storm passing through. I'm not meant for love. I proved that with Danny. An ache runs through me, squeezing my chest until I palm it away.

"We're too different," I whisper to myself, needing to hear the words spoken out loud. "You fall in love too easily, and something that feels this right is bound to be wrong." I'm not making any sense. One thing is certain. I'm no expert on love. What I do know, I learned from my relationship with Danny. He started our relationship under falsehood. I can't go through that again.

If Clay and I are willing to lie about our relationship to get ahead in life, then what else would we be willing to lie about as time goes on? The possibilities are endless, and I don't like where my thoughts take me.

I could call Clay and tell him everything. That there's no need to continue the fake relationship. The dinner tomorrow night doesn't really matter. It's just another falsity. What would happen if I started a job based on their assumption that I'm Clay's fiancee? Would they fire me once they found out the truth? I mean, they can't, but the doubt refuses to leave me alone.

"Call him and tell him." I search my pockets before remembering that I left my phone in the unit. It's probably for the best. I'd rather not be that woman who ends things over a text. We can have a real conversation soon enough. I just have to keep my defenses up and make sure I don't back down at the last minute.

"Kat!" Rex bellows my name. "Watch me. Kat, look what I learned."

It's impossible to be gloomy with Rex around. His cheerful exuberance lifts my spirits even before I turn.

His legs churn, spitting out sand in every direction. Once he knows I'm watching, he jumps and kicks one leg out and lands on his feet again. "Did you see? It's just like that movie. I can kick like him. Mom says I can join karate when we get home." He pushes hair back from his face and skids to a stop in front of me.

"That's awesome." I step out of the water and drop onto the hot sand. "Show me again."

Rex is happy to comply, and I need the distraction. Pam and Dalton wander down the beach hand in hand.

I wave to let them know I'll watch Rex and they shout their thanks. There's something about this group of guests. They almost feel like family. It's as ridiculous a thought as me falling in love with Clay, but a part of me wishes they didn't have to leave Nantucket.

CLAY

Dusk settles over the mainland dock as the last few travelers disembark the ferry. A chill of evening air brushes my neck, making me shiver. I pull my jacket closer around me, scanning the crowd for any sign of Kat. I texted her that I'll meet her here. My stomach coils—she hadn't replied back. Has she changed her mind about dinner?

I check my phone for any messages, but there's nothing. Frustration bubbles inside me. What if she doesn't show up? She wouldn't do that to me, would she? Kat seems reliable, but I could be all wrong about her.

Just as I'm resigning myself to the idea of attending the dinner alone, I spot her on the ferry, hesitating at the top of the ramp. Relief floods through me, but it doesn't last long when I find uncertainty clouding her expression. She catches my eye and gives me a small wave, a tiny smile tugging at the corners of her lips.

I make my way through the dispersing crowd toward her, my heart pounding in my chest. "Kat," I call out when I reach her. "You made it."

She nods, but there's a hint of something else in her eyes, something unspoken. "Yeah, I did," she replies softly, her gaze flickering away from mine.

Has something happened to upset her? I gently touch her arm.

She takes a deep breath. "Sorry, I'm not feeling myself lately. Maybe I'm nervous about tonight."

I place an arm around her shoulder and squeeze her into my side "You'll be great. You have nothing to be nervous about."

Her posture stiffens and she inches out of my hold. "Thanks. You're right. I'll be fine."

Her words contradict her body language. Did I do something?

"My car is this way." I point to the parking lot.

Her hands are occupied clutching at her purse, so I don't take her hand. We're not officially dating and maybe the kiss was one sided after all. I was the one who had initiated it.

The ride to Tony's house stretches to an eternity. Kat doesn't say much. If she acts like this at dinner, I doubt she'll get another client.

I open the car door for her and offer my hand. She takes it which kind of surprises me from the cold shoulder she's been giving me.

Kat studies me and smiles. "Got to keep up the act."

I blink, but quickly return a smile. "Yeah. Thanks for playing along a little longer."

Tony's wife, Michelle, greets us at the door and leads Kat and me to the dining room, adorned with elegant decor. The table is set with crystal glasses, linen clothes, and an array of dishes covered in foil. Roasted meats and garlic override my senses and my mouth instantly waters. My tummy grumbles and Kat looks down to my belly and her lips quirk sideways.

Michelle introduces us to Susan, a podiatrist who's expanding her business with a second clinic downtown. Her fiery red hair matches her bold personality, and she regales us with stories from her podiatry clinic that soon have us all in stitches while we casually help ourselves to the food laid out before us.

Kat relaxes in Susan's animated company, her laughter ringing out. It's so good to see this side of Kat again. Although I'm a little jealous that I'm not the one making her laugh.

Now's a good time to play it up a little for Tony. Kat and I are a couple in love, about to get married, so we should show affection.

I scoot my chair a little closer, ready to make my next move. I'm not that great at boyfriending, since I've not had many relationships. A few dates here and there, but not anything substantial to speak of.

Before I can do something romantic and spontaneous, Susan leans in closer to Kat, her eyes sparkling. "Let me tell you about the time I hired an admin assistant from Fiverr who mixed up 'corns' with 'coins' on the invoice," she chuckles.

Kat nearly spits out her water, but instead covers her mouth and gulps hard. "Oh, that's terrible. I promise you won't get those kinds of mistakes from me. I'm very meticulous."

Tony has a broad smile on his face. "Managing a podiatry clinic must be quite... feet-cinating."

I cringe at Tony's dad-joke. He's well known for them at the hospital. That and his poor coffee-making skills. I never accept a coffee from Tony. I learned my lesson early on when I first joined the team.

Kat is laughing but this time it's more of a polite, courtesy laugh. I rub circles over her back, lean in, and kiss her temple. "Having a good time?"

She stops smiling and seems to focus intently on me before saying, "Yeah, I am."

I brush some strands of hair from her neck and carefully place them over her shoulder, running my fingers like a comb to the ends. "Have I told you that you look beautiful tonight?"

Her lashes flutter and a pretty pink blush washes over her cheeks. Kat shakes her head slightly.

I tilt her chin with my thumb and meet her gaze. "Well, you do. You always do."

"Thanks," she says softly.

Susan interrupts our moment with another tale of how the Fiverr admin person sent out an invoice for a "poultry" treatment instead of podiatry. "I mean, imagine my client wondering why they were being billed for a chicken. How confusing is that?"

"Good thing you found out before more mistakes were made," Tony says. "That would hurt your reputation. With social media these days, it could have gone viral."

"My client was very understanding." Susan touches her chest. "Thank goodness."

She turns to Kat and winks. "I could use some extra help at the clinic. How are you with spreadsheets minus the foot puns?"

Kat's eyes widen, but then she grins. "I'm great with data and can look into what you need"

Susan nods approvingly. "Excellent. Let's schedule a formal interview soon."

Kat's smile grows wider. "I'd love that."

It's not long before we're saying our goodbyes outside Tony's house and walking down the driveway. Kat turns to me with a smile that reaches her eyes this time. "Thanks for tonight. It will be great to get the extra work."

"No problem, that's what friends are for." I gesture to the car, rush over to the passenger side opening the door for her. When I turn back around, Kat is still standing on the sidewalk, rubbing her shoulders and then shaking off some sort of daze. She hasn't been quite herself tonight. I thought everything went smoothly. Kat will gain another big client and Tony is more than impressed with my connections to Kat. She's a smart, fun and kind person. The perfect choice as my pretend fiancée. But maybe we will stay in contact and start something real. That's if my new position doesn't take over my life.

Chapter 15

"That's what friends are for." That's what he said the other night after dinner.

Clay's words rattle around in my head like shells rolling in the tide. What did he mean by that? Now's the time to ask for clarification.

I stare down at my phone, a lump in my throat that is impossible to talk around.

"I can't believe Liam and the others came back." Clay chuckles and I snap the phone back to my ear. "I worried there for a bit that Dalton would buy them all houses and they'd move to Nantucket for good."

"Not enough houses for sale." I answer automatically. Houses on Nantucket are not just expensive but they almost never go up for sale. What I want to say, the questions I want to ask, dance through my head. "You said the interview went well?"

"Yeah." He breathes out a short chuckle. "I was nervous at first, but that's normal for such a high-profile job, you know?"

No. I don't know. My career is nice and stable. It's also in semi high demand, but it's also a bit menial. There are not five different people itching for me to quit so they can have my job. I swallow and pace across my kitchen. The glass door reflects my image back at me, and I turn my head away from the shocked look stamped on my face.

"I really appreciate all your help. Sorry about Tony's jokes." He chuckles softly. "At least he didn't try to make coffee."

I smile at that but it doesn't hold. "I think I'll still get that job Susan offered."

Silence descends over the phone for so long that I check the screen. Seconds tick past before Clay speaks again. "I really enjoyed our time together." Something in his voice makes my pulse beat harder, but not in a pleasant way. This is more like the impending doom knell that happens in scary movies when the main characters do something stupid and get themselves killed.

That's it then. This is Clay's way of saying goodbye. I recognize the feeling of dread slithering up my spine. I knew it would end sooner or later, but I didn't expect this.

"Sorry that you had to put up with the charade for so long." His tone implies I should be grateful that it's over.

I grind my teeth and fight back the rush of emotion. "It's fine." A woman's catch phrase, and one that many men take at face value when they should be running for their lives.

What kind of fool does it make me that I had started to believe this was real? I stop and settle my arm over my stomach, propping the opposite elbow on my forearm and gripping the phone tight to my ear. I wait for him to say that he wants to make it real, but that is never going to happen.

I recognize the feelings welling up inside me and wince at my own stupidity. I'm no better than those characters who shout "who is it?" when the killer knocks on the door.

I like Clay. More than a little bit. I enjoyed our time together, even when things went completely sideways. I've never had this much fun dating someone.

"Thanks for putting up with my fake dating idea. Looks like I have the job in the bag." His low chuckle twists my gut into knots. "It's not official, but I feel good about it."

"I'm glad it worked out." Anger takes over the melancholy that slipped in. "I have to go."

"Oh." Clay pauses. "Sure. Thanks again."

"Yep." I force a brightness I don't feel into my voice.

The call ends without any kind of goodbye or a promise to talk again later, cementing my knowledge that Clay just broke up with me.

It's ridiculous. The whole thing was fake. I toss my phone onto the table and wrench the ring off my finger. Holding it up to the light, I examine the perfect stone and glossy band. I should be glad to have it off my finger. It's heavy and obnoxious. And if I'm being honest, I love it. I set the ring on the counter and walk away. I'll mail it back to Clay. Shoot. I don't even have his address on the mainland. Oh, but I can send it to Liam. His address is on file in the computer because he booked the trip.

My heart aches for what I've lost. Liam, Trina, Rex. They might come back to the resort for another vacation, but it won't be the same.

What about Clay? He won't be back. He's a workaholic who couldn't even stay away from his job for a week. My very real feelings for him mean nothing when I remember that he lied and manipulated everything to further his career. It's my fault. I went along with it.

I yank open the nearest cabinet and grab my box of tea, then slam the door closed. The sound echoes through the unit, reminding me once again that I'm alone.

"Not all men are liars." I march to the sink and add water to the tea pot, then set it on the stove to heat. "But I seem to find all the ones who are." I deserve better. My chest tightens and I rub the ache pounding in my temples. "It was all fake. You knew that. It's not all Clay's fault."

I want to blame him so that I can rant and rave that it's not fair. Yes, that kiss on the dock felt real, but it had nothing to do with his job. I let him kiss me, and I kissed him back. That's on me. A low grumble of thunder sounds in the distance, and I lift my head to stare out the window. "Yeah, you go ahead and rain." Nothing wrong with a good downpour to cleanse the earth. I could use a little cleansing of my own right now. If only I could purge my feelings for Clay as easily as the clouds release their burden of rain.

Chapter 16

CLAY

My phone buzzes in one hand as I struggle to balance a stack of pizza boxes in the other. Liam's name flashes on the screen.

I manage to swipe the phone with my thumb. "Yeah, I'm here already. Open the door," I say before he can even speak. "Before these pizzas burn a hole through my hand."

Liam cackles through the line before it clicks off. A moment later, the side door of the basketball court swings open to reveal my brother grinning at me. I stagger inside, the aroma of hot pizza spilling into the open space.

"Uber eats!" I yell, my voice echoing into the bleachers.

Liam's teammates ambush me. They grab the pizzas out of my hands like a pack of wild animals, hooting and hollering. My back and shoulders are subject to vigorous slaps that remind me of the end of a Chinese massage. I'm pretty sure my skin matches the color of the tomato sauce on those pizzas.

Before I can follow the guys to dig in, Liam grabs my arm. "How's things with Kat?"

I shrug. "Good, I guess. I haven't spoken to her for a while."

"Why not?" he asks.

"She must be busy."

Liam rolls his eyes. "You're not great with relationships. Have you called her?"

"Yeah, last week."

"I thought you liked her, wanted to date her for real."

"I do."

"So have you told her that?"

I sigh and run a hand through my hair. "I haven't found the right time or words."

Liam gives me an exasperated look. "Dude, you're overthinking it. Just be honest with her."

"I know, I know," I say, rubbing the back of my neck. "It's a little . . . complicated."

"How so?"

I hesitate before finally admitting, "She's been distant lately. I don't want to push her away by telling her how I feel too soon."

"What was the last conversation about?"

I run the dialogue through my head. "I told her, 'Sorry you had to put up with the charade for so long.' She responded with, 'It's fine.' Then I said, 'Looks like I have the job in the bag.'"

Liam frowns. "And what did she say after that?"

"She said, 'I'm glad it worked out.'"

Liam slaps me on the side of the head.

"Ouch!" I rub my scalp. "What's that for?"

"You dummy. She's not fine. When women say, 'it's fine', it means the opposite. It means you're in deep poop."

I massage my forehead—my brain hurts. I'm totally confused. This is why I don't date. How is a man supposed to understand their partner if they say one thing and mean the opposite? Is there an instruction booklet that explains this secret language? Even if there was a book, would men even read it? We can't even bring ourselves to ask for directions.

"Are you sure?" I ask.

"Yes. She hasn't called you since. You haven't made it clear of your intentions, and she's likely moved on thinking it's all over."

Dang it. This isn't how I wanted things to end between us. Maybe it started as an idiotic ploy, but the way I've come to feel about Kat is anything but fake.

Does she have any idea how bright her smile makes my day? How the easiness around each other makes me feel connected to her? That being my fake fiancée was more of an excuse to spend more time together. When she came along, it showed me what I was missing.

With a sigh, I scrub a hand over my face. "You're right. I need to go see her. Find out where things are at."

"Do it today." Liam crosses his arms. "You've left it too long already."

"I will. After pizza." I give his arm a quick squeeze before hurrying off to join the team, who greet me with more cheers and whistles. I may be the pediatric surgeon who brings them pizza, but these guys are like family to me now.

I'm wolfing down a third slice when Liam reappears, a frown creasing his forehead. "Why are you still here?"

"Why are you so bossy when I'm the older brother?"

"I've got more experience in relationships, and you have no clue. Someone has to help your poor helpless soul."

"Gee. Thanks for having faith in me." I lift my palms. "I'm going. I'll catch the ferry and tell Kat how I feel."

Liam playfully messes my hair, which is aggravating as heck. I resist the urge to punch his arm, considering he has a whole team of basketball players who could easily jump me and send me crashing through the floor.

KAT

A rap of knuckles on my front door draws my attention, and I hurry from the stove after a quick check that nothing will boil over or burn while I'm away. Maybe Aunt Marg brought me some yummy treats from the resort kitchen. She's been pushing food at me like I'm a half-starved child.

Grinning in anticipation, I twist the knob and pull the door open. Bright light blinds me for a few seconds. The sight of Clay rushes through me. "You're not who I expected." I'm being surly and irritable, and I think I have every right. "What are you doing here?" I fold my arms and try to stare down my nose at him. Not easy since he's taller and I'm too surprised to give it much effort.

He inches his hands into his pockets and rocks on his heels as he stands in my doorway. An uncertain look squints his eyes. "I came to see you."

"Why?" Shock forces the word out. "You could have called. Should have called, actually." It unsettles me to be surprised by him like this. I thought I'd never see him again. "Do you need another pretend date?"

His showing up out of the blue like this is too much like Danny. Fear attempts to weasel its way into my body. Danny's gone. I haven't seen him in weeks. Not since the fake proposal. The reminder of our fake relationship cuts through my fear and lifts my chin.

"Are you mad at me?" He sounds incredulous as he takes a step forward. "Liam was right."

I very nearly slam the door in his face. "What does that mean?" I've asked him three questions and not gotten a single answer yet. I back into the living room with Clay following me.

He closes the door, and there's a single second when worry takes hold.

I remind myself that I'm safe with Clay. He lied and manipulated, but he's not dangerous.

"I talked to Liam after our last chat. He seemed to think that your 'Fine' meant something different. I took it at face value. But this isn't fine." He motions at me while frowning.

He talked to Liam about me? I can't decide if I'm flattered or annoyed. Both. He had no right, but knowing that he was thinking about me has a strange effect on my anger. I lower my arms and turn my back on him. "I'm in the middle of cooking." It's a clear dismissal, but instead of leaving, Clay follows me into the kitchen.

He's never been inside my unit before, and it makes my nerves jump. It's my parents' place, with all their stylistic choices on full display, but it's like a second home to me. I'm comfortable here with Mom's checkered tablecloth covering the round table and Dad's rubber boots resting upside down on the boot rack.

The pot on the stove bubbles and hisses when tiny droplets spill over onto the glass top. I turn down the eye and pick up the noodles.

"What are you making?" Clay's right behind me, his presence as solid as the walls closing us off from the world.

I shrug and drop a handful of noodles into the pot. "Spaghetti."

"My favorite." He rolls up his white shirt sleeves. "Can I help?"

"No." I answer before I can think. "You never said why you're here." My pulse flutters with the thought that he came back to tell me he has feelings for me. I shove that thought aside and focus on stirring the noodles before they clump.

"I needed to talk to you face to face." Clay's voice is quiet at my back. A cabinet door opens and he riffles around.

"What are you doing?" I ask as I spin to face him.

"Looking for sauce ingredients." He's shoulders deep in the pantry, his voice muffled by the wooden walls. "Or even canned."

"Get out of my stuff." This is the last straw. I grab the back of his shirt and pull. His head knocks against the bottom of the door, but I refuse to feel sympathy. "You can't drop in like this." My voice shakes, and I hate myself for the moment of weakness. "This isn't right. This is my house, my space. You can't..." I inhale until my trembling eases. "You're acting like Danny right now."

Clay's entire body freezes. His eyes widen so much it's almost funny. "I..." He searches my face, and whatever he sees there causes him to take a step back. "I didn't think about that. I'm sorry." He steps back again. "I'll go."

He does exactly that, getting as far as the front door before I call out. "Why did you need to see me when you've already ended things?"

"Ended things?" Confusion laces his voice. "What do you mean?"

"You made it clear when you called that we were done. You said that it was nice pretending together, then you hung up." I clench the wooden spoon in a tight fist.

Clay stands at the door, his hand on the knob and his face stricken.

"Since you can't seem to make up your own mind, I'll do it for us both. It's over, Clay. I won't be jerked around. I went through enough of that with Danny. I won't let myself go down that road again."

"Kat." He breathes my name like a prayer.

I'm fired up and ready to go. I've dealt with deceitful men before. If I let him convince me that he meant no harm, I'll regret it later. I use my fear to fuel my voice. "There's no need for anything else between us. Not even friendship. You don't need me to help with your job." I don't know if they ever made it official. Is that why he really came? Did he need one more 'date' to convince them. Well, too bad. I'm done pretending. I breathe in deep and meet his stare. "Thanks for helping me with Danny. We're even now."

"That's all this was to you? You were playing along to repay me for helping you?" His voice is soft, sounding almost regretful.

I jerk my head in a nod. "That's what we agreed on." I need to push him away for good. There's only one sure way to do that. I'll deal with my self regret later, when I'm alone. "For the record, I regret it. We never should have lied to help you get that job. I'm glad things worked out for you, but I'm done." The spoon slashes through the air with a whistling wave.

Clay stands there another second, then twists the knob and walks out. His head droops and he looks away from me as he closes the door.

I wait until he passes the window, his shoulders and spine rounded forward in defeat, before I move to the door and lock it. I feel terrible, even though I knew it had to be said.

The whole thing was a lie that I let myself believe. Clay never cared about me. And the only way I'll get rid of my feelings for him is to cut him from my life completely.

I head back to the kitchen and turn off the stove. I can't eat. My stomach writhes with nausea and bitter bile climbs the back of my throat. Clay is not Danny.

Knowing that doesn't stop the unease clawing through me.

Chapter 17

CLAY

I stare at the patient file in front of me, but it might as well be a page from a Dr. Seuss book for all the sense it makes to my scrambled brain. My thoughts can't let go of Kat, with all the "what ifs". I let out a dramatic sigh and slump over my desk. Would anyone notice if I crawled under it for a quick nap?

Snap out of it, buddy. You've got snotty-nosed kids to attend to today. Boogers to wipe and lives to save. Priorities.

But the heaviness in my chest refuses to dissipate. Every minute detail keeps resurfacing, each misstep and lie compounding the gut-wrenching ache. If only I could go back and come completely clean from the start instead of digging myself deeper into a pit.

The fake relationship thing was stupid from the beginning. Pure arrogance blinded me to what mattered—her feelings. How could I have been so foolish to risk losing out on a possible future with Kat?

A soft knock at the door startles me out of the painful reverie. I push my palm into my eye socket to stop the burn as Dr. Kessler pokes her head in, regarding me with concern.

"Everything okay, doctor? You look a bit . . . off today." Her gaze travels pointedly to the untouched stack of files on my desk.

"I'm okay, just a little out of sorts." I cough, attempting to force a cheerful expression. "Dealing with some . . . personal matters. Shall we begin our rounds?"

The older doctor's eyes soften with understanding. "Is everything okay with you and your fiancée?"

How did she figure it out? Is it written on my forehead or something? — *Break-up alert. Handle with care.*

Does Dr. Kessler have that motherly six sense? I always found it weird how my mom would know when I was hiding something. I tense for a beat before giving a solemn nod. There's no point denying it—the doc will see straight through me.

Kessler crosses the room to give my shoulder a comforting squeeze. "If you need to take a mental health day, don't be a hero, son. We all go through troubles at some point."

Warmth rushes through me at her empathy, a stark contrast to the callous ambition that's ruled my life for too long now. I shake my head, mustering a more genuine half smile. "I appreciate that but keeping busy is probably for the best right now. Work will be a welcome distraction." I pause with a flicker of new resolve. "And it'll give me time to figure out how to fix this mess I've made."

Dr. Kessler studies me a moment before giving an approving nod and patting my arm.

"Relationships can be tough. Don't lose hope, Clay. If it's meant to be, you'll work it out together." With an encouraging smile, she turns and heads for the door, but pauses and glances over her shoulder. "I'll start the rounds, take your time," she says, leaving me to absorb her wise advice.

As I gather the neglected files with a steadier hand and make my way out into the pediatric ward, a seed of possibility takes root—a chance to fight for the amazing woman I carelessly let slip through my fingers.

Kat needs space and doesn't want to hear me out, but when she's calmed down, I can try to make things right. For once in my life, a woman is infinitely more important than any professional pursuit. I was content being single all this time, but since Kat's light shone into my life, losing her isn't an option I want to accept.

KAT

"What in the ever-loving world were you thinking?" Tim stalks toward me, the wind tearing through his hair and standing it on end.

My cousin Tobias trails along behind him. "Yeah, Kat. What gives? You ruined my golf game."

I stay sprawled on my beach towel, my arms propped behind my head. "Nice to see you too." I roll my eyes at Tobias, though he can't see. "Sorry, Toby, but you can't blame me. I didn't ask Tim to come."

Tim flops onto the sand beside me with a grunt and a growl. "Don't give me that."

"What?" I try to sound innocent, but it's not working. Tim knows me too well, and nothing can stop him once he gets like this. "Where's Kayla?"

"Talking to Mom." He pokes me in the ribs until I squirm away. "You called and left me a vague voicemail about that doctor guy. Said that things were over and for me not to worry."

I inch up onto my elbows. "Yeah, so? I thought you should know since you were worried when you found out about the whole fake relationship thing."

"Who pretends to date someone?" Tobias sinks onto the sand and flops onto his back, crossing his arms over his eyes. "Better to stay single. Play it safe."

Poor Tobias. He's had it rough these last few years in the dating world. He's sounding as cynical as Tim before Kayla.

Tim glares at Tobias but is ignored. "I was worried about you." He pokes me again, harder this time. "You give away your heart like it's replaceable. I worried you wouldn't be able to keep your emotions out of the game you were playing. Turns out I was right."

"So what if you were." I'm grumpy and irritated because he is right. We both know it, and it annoys me to no end that he can see right through me. "It's not a big deal. Clay was grateful that I helped him get the job. He got rid of Danny for me. We're even."

Tim's heavy stare stays in place.

I turn away but I still feel it burning into the back of my head. I miss Clay. There's no way around it. Even after sending him away, I can't stop thinking about our kiss. About us and the potential we had together. Doubt creeps around the edges of my thoughts, chewing away at my decision. What if I was wrong?

"Go ahead," I mutter when the silence stretches too long.

"What?" Tim sounds innocent, but there's a thread of steel in his voice that never completely goes away. "Tell you I told you so?"

I flip onto my side and face him. "It's what you want to say."

A muscle ticks in his jaw and he draws his knees up until he can rest his arms on them. "I thought about it. But what's the point? It won't make you feel better, and since I'm a reformed man and all that, I no longer take pleasure in proving I'm right."

"Then you'll be out of a job." I scoff and roll into a sitting position. "You love proving you're right."

"Not like this." He stares out across the water. "I never wanted to see you hurt, Kat. That's why I didn't want you to put yourself in this situation."

"Don't do like me." Tobias never moves his arms from his face. He rolls his feet from side to side, digging little trenches. "It takes time to heal. Make sure you give that to yourself. You need lots and lots of time. Alone."

Their concern warms me even more than the blistering sun. I angle the umbrella to shade me and Tim and throw my arms around his neck. "I like this new you." I almost joke about this new Tim but hold back so I don't risk hurting his feelings or making him withdraw into that old persona. "Did you come all the way here to check on me?"

He pats my arms where they hang around his neck and his body tenses a split second before he grins. "And to have a weekend away. Promised Kayla we'd go wind surfing."

"Oh boy. I'd pay to see that." I kiss his cheek even though he grumbles about it and sits back on my towel. If anyone will understand, I think it's Tim. I brace for his possible annoyance and spill my guts. "I miss him, Tim. I'm disappointed in myself for falling in love with him, and I wish things had worked out." It's a ridiculous idea that Clay and I could be a couple after all the duplicity. I've told myself that over and over again, but that kiss. That one kiss lingers with enough fire to burn through many of my objections. Surely that was real.

"Don't worry about Clay." Tim scowls down at the sand and digs his bare heels into the ground. "I'm going to have sand everywhere."

"Excuse me?"

Tim motions at his legs. "I've been out here half an hour and I'm already covered in sand. How does it get everywhere? I'm itching in places nobody should itch."

"Not that." I wave away his complaints. Sand is part of the deal here. You either learn to live with it or you go somewhere else. "What did you mean about Clay? There's nothing you need to do. Stay out of it."

"Right. Okay." He agrees too easily, but he stands and holds out his hand. "Come on. Mom wants you back at the house. She said something about you helping Ellie."

I groan and flop onto my back. "Your mom thinks I'm heartbroken and that the best thing for me is to keep busy."

"Busy is overrated." Tobias digs in deeper. I swear the man is part starfish the way he works his way into the sand. Maybe a crab too from the way he's talking. "I prefer long days on the golf course."

"We'll go golfing later." Tim barks at Tobias. "It won't hurt you to spend some time with family and get over yourself." He faces me and his expression softens. "You are heartbroken. And that is the best thing for you." Before I realize what he's doing, Tim grabs me by the waist and throws me over his shoulder. "Now stop moping and join the family. We're playing charades tonight." His voice lifts in a falsetto of fake amusement. "I can't wait."

I laugh and slap his back. "You can tell them you hate charades."

"Yeah." He bounces me hard enough to push all the air from my lungs. "But I like watching them play. Nathan is horrible." Now he sounds like the Tim I know. He still finds joy in seeing Nathan be bad at something. It is pretty funny though. Nathan can't act to save his life. We all end up laughing until we can't breathe.

Maybe Tim's right about that part. Maybe it is time I stop moping and wishing for things I can never have. Clay is back on the mainland living his best life with the job he's always wanted. I'm busier than ever thanks to the new contract. There's a chance it might lead to another with the hospital where Clay works. I can't handle seeing his name and billing his clients, or the thought of seeing his messy doctor scrawl every day.

Tim slings me to the ground but keeps his arm around my waist until my head stops spinning and I can stand on my own.

Kayla stands on the porch with her hands on her hips. "Are you abusing your cousin?"

"Nope." Tim whacks my shoulder with a smirk. "She needed to be knocked out of her funk."

"Oh, I know all about the funk." Kayla's grin rounds her cheeks and she jumps off the porch into Tim's arms. He swings her up to his chest and holds her close.

"For the record, I was enjoying my funk." I grumble and move past them.

Tim ruffles my hair like I'm five years old again. "Keep telling yourself that. One day, you'll believe it."

I wish. I'm glad that Tim found Kayla, and she stuck around to see him through his anger and resentment. He came out a better man for it all.

I recall a saying Aunt Marg told me once. Something about fire making some things stronger even as it destroys other things. It's a twisted metaphor, but I understand it more now than I did back then. This whole thing with me and Clay will make me stronger as long as I make it through the burning.

Looking at Tim's smiling face, I remember that he didn't actually agree to leave Clay alone. I need to extract a promise from him before he heads back to the mainland.

Chapter 18

CLAY

As I enter my office, I do a triple take and almost trip over my own feet. Tim Jones is lounging in my chair like he owns the place.

"How did you even get in here?" I sputter. "And more importantly, what on earth are you doing in my chair?"

I snatch the clipboard from his hands and find his name listed as my next patient. I rub the back of my neck. "You don't have any kids. How did you end up on my appointment list?"

With a smug look on his face, Tim taps his temple. "It's not what you know, it's who you know."

The light bulb flashes in my mind. Of course, it must be Nurse Anna. Tim's partner, Kayla, knows Anna and they were chatting at the picnic like long lost friends. Why is Anna in on this?

I sigh and mutter, "Can I have my chair back?"

Tim nonchalantly slides out of my seat like a slippery eel and into the swivel chair opposite my desk.

I shuffle papers, stalling as I gather my thoughts. He's not a patient, so why is he here, arms crossed and staring daggers?

I clear my throat. "What, uh, what can I do for you today?"

He scoffs. "Oh, you know exactly why I'm here, Clay." My first name sounds like a curse word on his lips. "I want to talk about Kat."

A rock forms in my belly, grounding me to earth.

Tim leans forward and palms his fists on top of my desk. "How could you use my cousin as a means to impress the hospital board, all for a title? Head of Pediatric Surgery." He spits out the phrase as if the job is equal to that of a trashman and not one that saves lives.

I swallow hard. I knew if the fake relationship got out, there would be consequences. But I justified it—I deserve that promotion. I worked hard to be the best pediatric surgeon on staff.

"Now just wait a minute," my voice wavers. "Kat agreed to the whole thing. It was mutually beneficial . . ." I trail off at the fiery anger simmering in Tim's eyes.

"Cut the crap, Clay. You manipulated her to serve your ego-driven interests. She's vulnerable. And using people is never okay."

His words hit me like a slap in the face. When he puts it like that . . . did I guilt Kat into helping me in return for protecting her from Danny? Have I become so ambitious that I would take advantage of others to rise to the top?

Tim shakes his head in disgust. "You lied to the hiring committee and took advantage of my cousin, all for the sake of status and more income. How could you stoop so low? That promotion should go to someone with integrity."

Hot shame rises up my neck. What have I done? He's right—deceiving the board and using Kat was not only stupid but also unethical. I'm a good surgeon, but I let my pride blind me.

"Tim, . . . I totally agree," I stammer. "I acted like a jerk, and Kat deserves better."

Tim sighs, unfolding his arms. "I appreciate you recognizing your error. Now end things with Kat cleanly. No more lies or stringing her along." He fixes me with a hard look. "And if you have any conscience at all, you'll come clean to the board about what you did."

I nod slowly. The shame burns through me, but I know what I need to do. "You're right. I'll fix this." Meeting Tim's eyes, I say with full sincerity, "Thank you."

A flicker of surprise passes over Tim's expression before it hardens again. "Don't thank me. Just do the right thing." He stands abruptly. "I'll be checking in with Kat, and if I find out you gave her any more trouble . . ." He leaves the threat hanging as he turns to go.

With my stomach in knots, I whisper to the empty room, "I'm sorry…" To Kat, to Tim, and most of all, to myself—for losing my way. But that's enough. It's time I reclaim my senses, and my integrity, no matter the cost. Even if I miss out on what I've been working toward for so long.

The hospital phone beside my computer rings, breaking me from my remorse. Clearly, my common sense took a vacation when I blurted to Tony that Kat was my fake fiancée.

I pick up the phone and automatically reply, "Clayton Ashley's office."

"Clay. We've come to a decision." Tony's voice remains neutral. "Can you make some time to come and see me?"

I'm free now. Tim's appointment or false appointment didn't take the full thirty minutes. He whirled in and out like a tornado. A man of few words and the ones he chose cut deep to the heart.

"I have twenty minutes now. Shall I swing by your office?"

"See you soon." He hangs up, leaving me guessing.

Have I got the position or not?

The trek to Tony's office seems like an endless marathon, my thoughts running wild with potential outcomes. Will he offer me a promotion? Or another cup of his stale coffee from his camping percolator kit? He never stops bragging about how much of a bargain it was.

The anticipation is killing me as I try to catch my breath from speed-walking a million corridors. Who designs these buildings anyway? Don't they realize hospitals are generally for sick people? So make it harder for them, yeah, flawless logic.

Finally reaching Tony's office, I knock lightly on the door before entering. Tony, Ms. Pembroke, and Dr. Arnold look up simultaneously.

"Clay, that was quick. Did you catch a whiff of what was brewin' and sprint down here?" Tony asks, motioning for me to take a seat. "Want a coffee?"

I touch my throat, anxiety pressing air from my lungs. "Tony, I need to explain something—" I nod a greeting to the board members. "—to you all."

Their response is a consensus of wrinkled noses as if I've emptied my bowels of toxic gas.

As I unravel the web of lies that has brought me to this moment, Tony's expression shifts from curiosity to concern. Disappointment creeps into Dr. Arnold's eyes as he listens intently to my confession.

When I finish speaking, there is a heavy silence in the room. Tony leans back in his chair, steepling his fingers as he contemplates my words.

"Clay," he finally says, his voice grave. "What you've done is unacceptable. The board values honesty and integrity above all else. You should know that."

I nod solemnly, fully aware of the consequences of my actions. "I'm prepared to face whatever repercussions come my way." I massage the tightness from my jaw.

Tony studies me for a long moment before sighing heavily. "I appreciate your honesty in coming forward. It takes courage to admit when we've made mistakes."

He leans forward, fixing me with a stern gaze. "But ..."

I swallow hard, bracing myself for what comes next.

"We're not offering you the position because of your relationship status. That would be discriminatory."

My jaw drops. Did he just say they are offering me the Head of Pediatrics?

"You've earned the position on your own merits. There's no other surgeon that has your level of skill in your department. You have an unblemished procedural record. Zero mortality rate, no post-surgery complications reported, and no malpractice claims."

I palm my cheek and drag it across my mouth. "Thank you," I mumble.

He gestures to me. "Thank yourself. You're a hero in many children's eyes. To hundreds of families. Plus, you've sacrificed a lot of your personal life. How could we deny you this position for not having a partner when you've put others before yourself? Clay, you of all professionals need to be recognized and rewarded for your years of focused dedication."

I tunnel my fingers through my hair, probably making me look like a crazy scientist. I'm feeling a little crazy about achieving my dream even though I made a terrible mistake.

I need to make it up to Kat or all this doesn't matter if she doesn't forgive me and give me a chance to earn her trust. I want to date her for real this time.

I place my hands together and bow in a namaste mudra, totally brain-fogged on who I am and what just happened. "Thank you. Thank you." I lift my chin. "Can I be dismissed?" I say like I'm a school kid and I'm busting for the bathroom. "I need to go to my next appointment. Then I need to see Kat and tell her the good news. After I apologize."

Ms. Pembroke smiles generously. "I think that is wise, young man. By the way, I could tell that you have real feelings for her. The way you looked at Kat wasn't fake. You had admiration and couldn't take your eyes off her. Smitten. That's the word I was looking for." She places a hand on the side of her chin. "Adorable."

"Uh. Yep. That's me. Adorable." I laugh. With my chest eased of heaviness, I lift a hand and wave. "Wish me the best, then." And with that, I leave with a renewed sense of hope. A clean slate.

Chapter 19

KAT

Finally. I snap my laptop closed, remove my bluelight blocking glasses, and rub my aching eyes. My back protests when I stand and stretch with arms over my head. A buzzing from my phone draws my attention off to the side. It's on silent, so the call rolls to voicemail before I realize Tim's calling. I shrug and roll my head side to side with my hands on the back of my neck like a brace. If I'm going to work this long at a desk, I might need to invest in a standing desk and maybe even a treadmill. Sitting all day is going to make me lazy. And Nantucket is too pretty not to have the energy to explore.

Another buzz tells me Tim's finished his voicemail. I swipe my phone up and tap the message, putting it on speaker as I grab what I need and head outside.

Tim's voice is low and grouchy. "Kat. You're supposed to answer when I call. You know I hate voicemail."

I grin because he's right, and because I would have ignored the call even if I'd seen it in time. I rarely get a chance to annoy Tim, so I get my hits in where I can.

He lets out a long exhale. "I saw Clay today. You won't have to worry about him anymore. I took care of it. You won't have to worry about him."

My heart stops. Like frozen in ice nothing is moving, my body might as well be an iceberg, frozen. I can't move or even think.

"Clay won't be bothering you. You can move on now." He says it nonchalantly, but the steel underlying the tone sticks my feet to the sand.

The call ends. No goodbye. Nothing. Just *click*. "What did you do?" The instant the words leave my mouth, I'm in motion again. I jab Tim's name on my phone...and it goes straight to voicemail. The little heathen has either turned off his phone or he's deliberately ignoring me and sending me to voicemail as punishment. With Tim, it could be either. Growling out my frustration, I bolt back to my house and burst through the front door. Wallet. Keys. Phone. The phone stays in my hand as I spin on my heel and lock the door behind me while tapping Clay's cell number. It rings three times and I growl in frustration and end the call when his voicemail clicks on. I'm starting to understand Tim's annoyance with people missing calls. Who else can I call? I don't have Liam's number. My heart beats in my throat, making it hard to breathe. I run toward the ferry dock as fast as my poor legs can carry me.

If I can't get hold of Tim or Clay on the phone, I'll have to track one of them down in person. I skid to a stop in front of the ticket office and work to bring my wheezing down to something less than frantic. My throat and side aches from the impromptu run but that's the least of my worries. I google the hospital's number and step into line to buy my ticket. An automated voice rasps in my ear. "Thank you for calling Grace and Holmes Emergency Medical and Surgical Hospital. For English, press one."

The urge to scream roars up. I need to get to Clay and I'm hitting roadblock after roadblock. I tap one so hard my nail screeches across the screen. The automation goes through another list of prompts, one of which asks if I'm experiencing a medical emergency and if I am to please hang up and dial 911. Good grief. If they made these things any more difficult to navigate I might as well give up now. It's like they don't even want to talk to their patients. Finally, finally, I make it through the garbage and the monotonous voice starts listing the different hospital departments.

I reach the front of the line. The woman behind the counter frowns at me. I'm being rude using my phone while buying my ticket, but this is my priority and I smile an apology. "Emergency," I whisper when her face doesn't change. She rolls her eyes at my excuse but hands me my ticket.

I snatch it up and weave through the cluster of people blocking me from the door. Being out at the dock won't make the ferry appear any faster, but moving makes me feel better.

"If you would like to repeat this list again, please press pound." What? I blink and stare at my phone as I come to the realization that I missed the end of the message. Furious, I tap the pound key and wait for the whole thing to start over again. At this rate, I'll arrive at the hospital before I even reach Clay's office.

Nervous energy drives me to pace up and down in front of the rows of benches that line the water. A white fence keeps onlookers from tumbling down into the water, and several people stand around talking and taking pictures.

"For pediatric surgery, press five."

I've never moved so fast to press a button. The phone rings and rings. My hand tightens until my fingers throb. Just when I'm about to give up, a chipper, human voice answers. "Dr. Ashley's office, how may I direct your call?"

"I need to talk to Clay. I mean, Dr. Ashley." The tension in my throat makes my voice breathless and weak. "It's an emergency."

"Are you a patient?"

Grrrrr. More hospital protocol. "Not exactly."

"Are you calling about a patient of Dr. Ashley's? I can take a message, but I'm afraid I can't transfer you to Dr. Ashley's phone without more information."

I need to know if he's safe. The words almost blurt out, but I hold them back. In this situation, they could be taken as a threat, which would put the hospital on lockdown. What can I say to convince this woman to let me talk to Clay? "I'm his fiancee. I tried calling his cell but he's not picking up." Better she thinks of me as a crazy, potentially jealous, girlfriend than a psycho calling in a threat. "I wanted to send him a gift but wasn't sure what time would be best."

"Oh." The woman giggles and there's a nervous quality to it that lifts the hairs on the back of my neck. "I'm sorry, but all gifts go through our security protocol, so it's almost impossible to have something delivered at a specific time."

Drat. She's not buying it. "Okay. Well, could you at least put me through to his office so I can leave him a message?"

"I'm sorry, but office policy is rather firm on phone calls as well. Dr. Ashley's office phone is for patients only. I'm sure you understand."

"Yes. Thank you." It takes all my experience in customer relations not to rant at her. It's not her fault. I hang up as the ferry horn blasts to announce its arrival. Time has never passed as slowly as it does now. People disembark at a snail's pace that feels like it takes hours.

By the time I'm on the ferry and leaving Nantucket, I've dreamed up all sorts of terrible things that might have happened to Clay. I replay every word the woman said. None of them give me comfort. They don't reassure me that he's okay, because there's no way she would admit that he'd been hurt to a complete stranger. Especially over the phone. I stand on the upper deck, the same place I stood with Rex. My fingers dig into the rail as I will the ferry to move faster and rush down the steps when I spot the mainland.

I'm the first one off when we dock and run straight for the Uber I booked during the ferry ride over. "Grace and Holmes Medical," I pant. "The Hospital." I puff out the address and push sweat-dampened hair back from my face.

The woman behind the wheel lifts her eyebrows. "You need an emergency room?"

"No," I bark out, then hold out a hand in apology. "I'm going to see someone. It's very important that I get there quickly." I try calling Tim again with the same result as the previous five attempts.

She shrugs and pulls out onto the street. Everything blurs as tears prickle behind my eyelids. Clay might be hurt because of me. What did Tim do to him? I never considered him violent, but I'm the first to admit that he knows some seedy people who would be more than willing to have Tim Jones owe them a favor if they roughed up a doctor for him.

Please. Please. Please. Let Clay be all right. I can't imagine any other possibility.

My driver pulls me right up to the hospital doors and I manage a genuine "thank you" before I leap out and rush through the automatic doors. My eyes skip over the space. I need a directory. I spot it, a dull gray metal sheet listing all the specialties. Pediatric Surgery. Sixth floor. Great. My flip-flops slap loudly but I'm over caring. I hop into the elevator as the doors try to close, shoving my way between several men and women in scrubs. They look at me sideways but no one says anything. This is a hospital, after all. Strange in their world is someone walking in with a screwdriver sticking out of their scalp and asking for an antacid because they have heartburn. I billed a visit like that a year ago, and saw a few even stranger. A woman dressed for the beach slamming the number six button over and over like that will make the elevator go faster doesn't even register as strange, odd, or mysterious.

I bounce from foot to foot. The elevator stops at every single floor on its way up. Those who've been along for the ride with me whisper "good luck" when I throw myself into the lobby. Whew. Made it. I need to present as calm and collected when I approach the desk, but it's all I can do not to scream Clay's name.

A woman in blue scrubs lifts her head when I stop at her desk. "Can I help you?"

"I need to see Dr. Clay Ashley."

Something about my appearance must show my desperation. Maybe it's my eyes or the frazzled way I keep running my fingers through my hair, because her face falls into what looks like remorse. "I'm sorry. He's in surgery."

"What?" I stumble back from the circular desk.

She starts to rise but stops with her palms on the desk. "Are you family?"

I nod numbly. Yes. I'm family.

Her eyes soften. Oh, no. I know that look. That's the 'something terrible has happened so lets be nice to the people so they don't freak out' look. "Someone will be out to talk to you soon. Why don't you have a seat in the waiting room? There's coffee, tea, and snacks if you need something."

I nod again, unable to do anything else, and make my way to the waiting room. My mind spits out all the possible scenarios in rapid bursts.

Clay's hurt and he's in surgery.

Has anyone called Liam?

Why am I waiting here? If Clay is in surgery, he'll be on another floor. Where's the surgery floor?

The off white walls swim in and out of focus when I start pacing again. I can't keep still. And my hands shake too much to risk trying to hold anything hot.

CLAY

At last, I emerge from the operating room, exhausted but elated to have successfully completed a delicate spinal surgery on an eight-year-old patient. Peeling off my surgical mask, tension leaves my shoulders that I've carried for too long now—ever since the fake engagement and dishonest grab for promotion.

But I came clean to the board and, by some miracle, still managed to land Head of Pediatrics on my surgical skills alone. No more scheming or cutthroat ambition at the expense of others. Just hard work and doing right by the kids.

My thoughts derail completely as Kat jumps out from the waiting area, round eyes focused on me.

Without warning she rushes over, and throws her arms tight around my neck. "Thank goodness you're all right. I was so worried that Tim had arranged some mob to get you or something crazy," she says way too loud in my ear.

I freeze. What's she talking about? Oh, no. The look in Tim's eyes when he left my office. "Tim wouldn't—would he?"

She squeezes my neck harder. "I hoped not. Just he likely has connections and he used to be a different man before Kayla, but anyway, you're perfectly fine." She runs her hands over my bicep and nuzzles into my neck. Her lavender scent surrounds me, and I find myself grinning over her shoulder. Kat was worried about me. She still cares.

"Yep. I'm injury-free. Wasn't me on that table."

We slowly separate. Her hands linger on my shoulders and she scans my face intently. I meet her bright smile and all other sounds of the busy ward fade away for a second. I cup her cheek and draw her to my lips. An explosion erupts in my chest as she responds with desperate kisses. She missed me and I missed her. Missed this.

Maybe I will need surgery after all because kissing Kat messes with my once closed heart and organized life. She's opening me up and making space for herself and a possible future together.

A few playful whistles from passing nurses snap me from my daze. We spring apart, both flushing as colleagues call out cheeky comments.

"Get out of here with that smoochy smooch. Room 6B is free, if you need post-surgery tender loving care, Dr. Ashley."

"Is kissing allowed on duty, doctor? Think that's against policy procedures."

Kat covers her face before peeking at me through her fingers. "Oh gosh, I just mauled you at work. I'm so sorry, I don't know what got into me." She brushes a palm over my chest. "Must be the scrubs. Something about you in a doctor's uniform and saving lives like a superhero makes me lose control."

My heart lifts at her cute confession. Throwing professionalism aside, I chuckle and gently thread my fingers through hers. "Don't be sorry. I'm not complaining at all." Happiness rushes through me at what this could mean . . . assuming my past idiocy hasn't ruined everything.

Dr. Arnold steps out of the surgery room, wanders over and gives me a congratulatory pat on the back that nearly knocks me off balance.

"Our new Head of Pediatrics! What a flawless, meticulous spinal fusion—nice work, Clay."

Dr. Arnold winks roguishly at a mortified Kat. "And seems your personal life is shaping up too from that little display, eh?"

We both blush again. But Dr. Arnold just laughs. "Ah young love. Well, I won't keep you, but take your girl out for a celebratory dinner. My treat. If you go to Clancy's on Fifth Avenue, tell them I sent you and put it on my tab. They'll call to confirm, and it'll be all sorted." He squeezes my shoulder. "I'm proud of you for coming clean too. That was good of you to humble yourself at the risk of your career. We're surer than ever that we made the right choice to promote you."

He ambles off, leaving Kat staring at me. "Came clean? So you told them, and they still gave you the job?"

I rub my neck. "It's a long story but I was an ambitious jerk using you for career advancement. Until your cousin Tim set me straight," I say flatly. "How about we grab that dinner? If you'll still go with me? I'll tell you everything."

Her features soften into a gracious smile that lifts my spirits. "I won't say no to a free meal at Clancy's." She winks and loops her arm through mine. "And for the record, I like the real deal Clay even more."

My heart somersaults in my chest as I take her warm hand in mine, enjoying the certainty of her touch. I kiss her knuckles. "Good. No more faking. The real deal from now on."

Chapter 20

NINE MONTHS LATER...

CLAY

I take a steadying breath as I approach the pre-op room, giving myself a moment to mentally transition from concerned uncle to focused surgeon. Rex is waiting for me behind that door, understandably terrified about his upcoming procedure. It's my job to put him at ease.

With a gentle knock, I push inside and am immediately met with Rex's apprehensive brown eyes, so reminiscent of his mother's, who's sitting quietly beside him. The poor little guy looks impossibly small, swallowed up in the oversized hospital gown.

"Hey there, buddy." I greet him with an encouraging smile, sliding into the chair beside his bed. Up close, the slight quiver of his lip has my heart clenching. He's putting on a brave face for a five-year-old about to have surgery. "How's my favorite nephew doing?"

He manages a tiny half-smile at that, unconsciously clutching his stuffed dinosaur a bit tighter. "A little scared."

The small voice trips over the obvious understatement and the look of pure vulnerability he levels at me nearly undoes my composure. This fragile boy isn't just my "adopted" nephew—he represents the huge responsibility I have to every child under my care.

Pam folds her hands in her lap, her fingers fidgeting. This is tough for her too.

Clearing my throat past a lump, I gently ruffle Rex's sandy blonde hair. "This all seems scary, but you're being incredibly brave, Rex. I'm proud of you."

With these words of affirmation, he sits taller in the bed. "You think so?"

"Absolutely." I pat his hand. "And you know what else makes you super cool? You get to help take care of yourself in a really special way today."

Rex's forehead creases. "Huh?"

Leaning in closer, I shift into my best teacher mode and speak with a bright smile. "Well, you know how you have to do all those boring things every day like checking your blood sugar and having shots because of annoying diabetes? Today, we're putting in this nifty little pump that will do all that work for you. No more pesky shots."

His eyes widen as he processes the information. "No more owies?"

"That's right." I give his hand a playful squeeze. "I'll put a fancy pump right here . . ." I point to his abdomen, "which will take care of everything for you. How awesome is that?"

Relief and amazement register across Rex's features, and it fills me with a profound sense of purpose. Being able to watch apprehension melt into understanding like that—helping ease a child's suffering in any way—is what makes this job mean everything to me.

"That does sound pretty cool." Rex manages a tiny grin. He's adorable.

"It's so cool." I laugh, ruffling his hair again. "Plus, you'll get to pick out some fun stickers to cover up the little bandage when it's all done. What's your favorite dinosaur?"

At that, Rex's whole face lights up as he launches into an animated chat about his latest obsession with pterodactyls and stegosauruses. I engage enthusiastically, drinking in his bright-eyed excitement over something so simple.

We're immersed in our dinosaur detour that I barely notice the nurse slipping in to start getting Rex prepped for surgery. He's so at ease trading jokes and facts with me that he doesn't even flinch at the IV line being inserted.

Pride swells in my chest as Rex handles this daunting situation with courage. He's just a little kid—he shouldn't have to be dealing with a scary illness, undergoing an operation . . . and yet he's braver and stronger than most adults I know.

I'm acutely aware of how privileged I am to play even a small part in improving the quality of life for kids like Rex, giving them the best chance to overcome their struggles. More than a job, it's a calling—doing everything possible so no child has to suffer needlessly if I have the expertise and skill to help them.

Leaning in, I brush hair away from Rex's forehead and lock eyes with him. "I'm going to do everything I can to make sure your surgery goes perfectly smooth, and you'll feel all better in no time at all, okay?"

He nods resolutely, pure innocence shining in his eyes. "Okay, Uncle Clay. I trust you."

Those four simple words blow through me like a wrecking ball, stealing my breath. The magnitude of his utter reliance on me to take care of something so precious as his life . . . it's both terrifying and the greatest honor I could ever receive.

I hold back tears. I need to keep it together for Pam and Rex's sake. I pull Rex into one final hug, stroking his hair. "I love you, little man. You relax and let me handle the rest—you'll have those awesome stegosaurus stickers before you know it."

I wrap my arms around him tightly, struggling to contain the rush of feelings that are almost too much to handle. This is what it means to have a strong bond with family. It makes me long for my own family someday, and more than anything, I want Kat to be the mother of my children. I can only hope that she sees me as a good potential father. After all the time we've spent together, I've earned her trust. Now, I need to come up with a meaningful way to propose to her.

Maybe Rex can play a part and make it unique. Can I trust him not to mess things up? He's trusting me with his very own body. His life. He'd love to be a part of doing something special for his new Aunt Kat.

Decision made. Now I just need to work out the logistics.

KAT

I knock quickly on Clay's office door before twisting the knob and entering. He's told me I don't have to knock, and his nurse—the same one I spoke to on the phone—always lets me come through. But today is different.

Today Clay is checking on Rex after his insulin pump placement. I passed Pam and Dalton in the elevator, the two of them headed down to grab lunch while Rex visits with Clay.

Pushing the door open, I peek around it. "Is it safe to come in?"

Rex zooms around the room, his arms out like he's an airplane. "Vrrrrr." He bounds over to the nearest chair and leaps into it, then starts jumping up and down. "Hi, Kat. Look what I can do." He crouches down and spreads his arms wide.

Clay snags him around the waist. "No, sir. We talked about that. No jumping from the chair to the desk."

"Aw, man." Rex goes limp in Clay's arms. The relaxation lasts mere seconds before he stiffens his legs and holds his arms out again. "Spin me, Uncle Clay."

Clay lets out a sound that is half laugh, half sigh. "For a boy who just got his insulin pump put in, you sure are full of energy."

"It's the juice." Rex kicks his feet, the movement reminding me of when I first met him on Nantucket. He pats his side where the insulin pump is attached. "Mom says the stuff in here will make me feel better. It does."

Clay lifts his head and meets my eyes. I recognize the look as adorable exasperation. "It will make you feel better, but you are still a growing boy, and it does not make you invincible."

"Does that mean disappear?" Rex swivels his head around, twisting until Clay lowers him to the chair, where he pops up onto his feet and grabs Clay by the face. "Can you make me invi...visin..." He scrunches his nose. "What you said."

"We'll talk about that later." Clay tugs his tie, loosening it. "Don't you have something for Kat?"

Rex frowns and squishes Clay's cheeks until his eyes are tiny slits and his mouth is spread in a weird smile. "It's in my pocket."

Clay tries to talk, but Rex rolls his cheeks around the opposite direction until Clay takes Rex's hands and gently pulls them away. "Remember what we talked about?" he whispers.

Rex nods and grins at me over his shoulder. "Uh-huh." He whirls around and shoves a hand into his pocket. "Catch me, Kat."

Before I'm ready, Rex launches off the chair and flies through the air. I catch him and stumble back. "Oof."

Rex laughs, showing off a gap where he's lost a baby tooth. "You're funny too. Here." He uncurls his fingers and shoves his hand under my nose. "This is for you."

My eyes go crossed trying to make out the object in his palm.

Behind Rex, Clay smacks a hand to his forehead, his shoulders shaking with laughter.

"Do you like it?" Rex leans back and holds his hand up in front of my eye. "Uncle Clay says it's very, very, very, special. And I'm supposed to take good care of it. That's why it was in my pocket with my gummy bears."

"I see that." I focus on the glob of mangled colors in all their sticky glory. "Why don't you let Clay help us for a minute." I shoot him a desperate look and he takes Rex from me.

I pluck the mess from Rex's hand and motion over my shoulder. "Let's wash this off in the sink." I've never been happier that Clay has his own private bathroom in his new office. There's something firm in the middle of the goop and I stretch it out to get a better look.

My breath catches in my throat and I almost choke on air. "Clay?"

Rex slides from his arms, tugging Clay down by his tie. "You're 'posed to get on one knee. That's what Daddy says."

"Right." Clay grimaces. "Maybe we wash it off first."

"Can I still eat the gummy bears?" Rex asks.

"No." Clay and I answer at the same time, and Rex scuffs his shoes over the carpet.

"Fine." His lower lip pooches out.

I hold out my hand to him. "Come help me clean this up. Then we'll find you some new gummy bears." Unless...I give him a look that I picked up from Pam. "Rex, do you have more gummy bears in your pockets?"

"Uh..." He fists his hands deep in his pockets and walks backward, refusing to look at me or take my hand.

Clay's laugh startles Rex and he bolts behind Clay's desk.

"Go." Clay motions me toward the bathroom. "I'll take care of the candy monster under my desk." He closes the distance between us. "I saw this going differently in my head."

I tip my chin up and kiss his cheek. "It was sweet of you to include Rex. If this is what I think it is. Not smart, maybe, but sweet."

I make my way into the bathroom and wash the gummy bears off a silver engagement ring. A single, square stone sits in the center, and I realize it's almost identical to the first one Clay gave me. We returned that ring some time ago. The negative feelings I felt every time I looked at it soured my appreciation for the ring. This one, however. This one has my heart speeding a hundred miles an hour.

The ring glints brightly even in the low lighting and I turn to make my way back into Clay's office. Rex is nowhere to be found, and my gaze lands on Clay kneeling in front of the broad windows that offer a panoramic view of downtown. He holds up the empty box, a smirk tugging on his lips. "I love you, Kat. We got off on the wrong foot for a while, but these last months have shown me that there's no way I can live the rest of my life without you. Will you marry me?"

I slide the ring onto my finger while crossing to him. Like Rex, I grab his tie and pull, this time bringing him to his feet. "I'd like that very much."

His grin widens until our lips meet. The feel of him and knowing that he's mine is enough to give me goosebumps. Things will be different this time. We've both learned from our mistakes. We took our time getting to know each other, and the future is something I look forward to with anticipation instead of dread.

Knocks pound on the door. "Uncle Clay, can we come in now?" Rex bellows from the other side.

Quiet shushing slips through the cracks, telling me that Pam and Dalton are attempting to wrangle the tiny tornado.

I pull back from Clay and wrap my arms around his waist. "You can come in."

The door opens and Rex barrels in at full speed. "Did I miss it? Are you getting married?"

I hold out my hand, showing him the ring. "Yes, we're getting married."

Dalton leans toward us and lowers his voice to a stage whisper. "Make sure the cake is on a table that absolutely cannot fall over."

Pam backhands his shoulder, her cheeks pinking. She finally cracks a smile and explains, "Rex almost knocked over Trina and Liam's cake at their wedding."

Rex, completely ignoring the adults around him, scrambles into Clay's chair, plants his feet on the edge of the desk, and pushes himself backward. The chair spins and he laughs. The sound is so innocent and gleeful, so full of life.

That's what I want for my future. A mix of fun and frivolity to go with the serious moments.

Epilogue

ONE YEAR LATER...

KAT

It's hard to believe how things came together. I stand beside Clay and tip my head up, taking it all in. His smile is steady and true, a constant since our marriage. He might still lean toward overworking himself, but he's learning how to make boundaries so that his work doesn't eclipse his personal life.

Warm sunshine and the crowd in front of us creates a festive atmosphere.

Rex darts in and out among our family. Our family. I like the sound of that. Someday, Clay and I might have a child of our own. In the meantime, we've worked hard at achieving another dream.

Dalton slides an arm around Pam's waist and grabs Rex with the other, catching the boy in mid run and bringing him to a stop. Rex swivels to face us and grins, waving both hands in wide arcs. "Is it time yet?"

Clay shakes beside me with quiet laughter. "Yeah, buddy. It's time."

"Woohoo!" Rex jumps and pumps both fists into the air.

Off to the side, two news reporters take pictures. We've already been interviewed and the articles are ready to go. This is the last step, the official opening. Tobias stands along the edge, his camera in front of him as he clicks. He lowers the camera and frowns, then tilts his head toward a woman by his side.

She's too far away for me to hear, but the animated way she moves her hands is familiar. Why do I feel like I know her?

I wave at Tobias to get his attention. He nods that he sees me but grins at the woman. Annoyance pushes its way in. What was all that about playing it safe and protecting his heart by staying single? The look he's giving the woman is a dead giveaway that he's not following his own advice.

Clay holds up one hand and everyone falls silent. Well. Almost everyone. Rex tries, even covering his mouth with both hands, but he fidgets and hops in place.

Aunt Marg and Uncle Steve, Mom and Dad, and all the rest of my family mingle with Clay's family. We all fell into being one big family so fast that it still makes my head spin.

"Thank you all for coming out today. This is a long-awaited dream, and one that neither Kat nor I knew would come together the way it did." Clay's voice is warm and smooth. The Head of Pediatrics job is what sent us on this journey. Clay is a fantastic surgeon and a wonderful man to work for. He found out that the job he'd craved as the Head of Pediatrics came with less time in the operating room and more time in his office with stacks of paperwork.

This is the best of both those worlds.

Clay takes my hand and squeezes. "Clay and I are thrilled to officially open Ashley Pediatrics, a multi-doctor specialty clinic and surgical facility."

Cheers roar and everyone claps, filling the sidewalk and the surrounding area with noise. A few cars drive past, and more than one rolls down their window when they reach the stop sign and ask what's going on.

Tomorrow morning, we'll be front-page news. We've been advertising for months and already have several patients on the week's schedule.

Clay and I turn to face each other and step back, exposing the glass doors leading into our building. It's a surreal feeling, knowing this is our place. My background in billing, coding, and office management combined with his pediatric surgery skills means we have a lot of work ahead of us, but we both agreed that it's worth it.

The tall white building stretches high behind us. Off to the left, a catwalk attaches our building to the pediatric surgery wing on the other side. We did our best to cut down on confusion in navigating between spaces, but as soon as we began building, we realized that we needed to remain close to the hospital while also being a separate entity.

"Yay!" Rex tugs Dalton's hand. "Let's go see the fish."

Dalton pretends to resist, but he lets Rex haul him toward the door and inside.

Clay holds one door, while I hold the other, and we usher in our friends and family, along with several prospective clients that we've been talking to and who wanted to come see the place for themselves.

I've never seen an office have an opening like this before, but it's been exactly what we needed.

Tobias walks past, his brows furrowed and his lips moving in a mutter.

"Hey." I grab his sleeve and pull him to a stop. "What's wrong?"

"Nothing." His grip on the camera tightens.

I arch a brow. "Does this nothing have anything to do with the woman I saw you talking to?"

He clamps his lips together and grinds words between clenched teeth. "Leave it alone, Kat." He stalks off before I can say anything else. The woman has disappeared, and I still don't remember why she looked familiar.

Cool air brushes over my face. The last two people walk in and I take Clay's hand, leading him into the open waiting room. Colorful paintings dot the walls, and the floor is inlaid with a bright pattern that encourages kids to move around. A quiet room on my right offers parents and children the ability to get away from the lights and noise.

We've done all we can to accommodate every need. I squeeze Clay's hand. "Good work, Dr. Ashley."

He lifts my hand and kisses my knuckles. "I could not have done it without you."

We stand side by side, our staff coming to join us.

This is our future, and I wouldn't have it any other way. Clay and I found common ground in our love of caring for others. His caring heart drew me to him from the beginning, and the playful nature beneath the solemn exterior shows more than a giving heart. I love all the different parts of him and our relationship.

"Rex is trying to climb into the fish tank. Again." I pull him across the lobby with a laugh.

He pretends to scowl. "I told you the fish tank was a bad idea."

"Right. And your idea of a mini golf course out back was a good one?" I bite back the smile begging to break free. We've pretended to argue about this for months. "Thank goodness we went with fish and not turtles, or the poor things would be turned into golf balls."

"Don't give Rex any ideas."

Dalton scoops Rex away from the fish tank and the two of them rejoin Pam. I love seeing Rex comfortable enough here to be himself. That's what we want for all the children that come into our care, and that's what they'll get—a fun and safe place to be themselves.

Free Novella

GET *Fake Dating My Grumpy Billionaire Boss* the prequel to the *Nantucket Romantic Comedies* series when you join Taryn Daniels newsletter.

BEING MY GRUMPY BILLIONAIRE'S boss for a charity ball sounded simple enough. But now Dalton wants to teach me to waltz, and my two left feet have a mind of their own. Even though I've stomped his poor toes to a pulp, Dalton's determined to spin me around the ballroom flawlessly for the big event. Little does he know I've got butterflies doing backflips in my stomach that have nothing to do with dancing. Maybe I'm not as immune to his dreamy eyes and delicious cologne as I thought.

Oh boy. Fake-dating my boss is a bad idea...and what if the feelings become real? How can I work with him after that kiss? Especially when his interfering mother thinks I'm just after his money to support my little boy. With my heart and my son's at stake, I have to find a way to make this arrangement work without losing my job.

If you enjoyed The Proposal by Jasmine Guillory, you'll love the whirlwind of emotions in the sweet romantic comedy, Fake Dating My Grumpy Billionaire Boss. Be swept away to gorgeous Nantucket Island and experience heart-warming unexpected love.

Get your free copy from https://books.bookfunnel.com/cousinsofnantucket

More Books by Taryn Daniels

GET THE FIRST TWO BOOKS in the *Nantucket Romantic Comedies* series,

Amnesia on Nantucket and Love Unscripted.

Or check out the *Cousins of Nantucket series here:* https://books.bookfunnel.com/cousinsofnantucket

Please Leave a Review

YOU'VE MADE IT THIS far, so I trust you enjoyed the story. So others can find out what you liked about *Love on Call*, I'd love you to take a minute to leave a review. If you don't have a minute, a star rating is perfectly fine and still much appreciated!

Please post a review on Amazon and copy and paste it to BookBub or Goodreads. If you haven't signed up for my newsletter, you can follow me on any of these platforms to find out when the next book is released.

Happy Reading,
Taryn Daniels

About the Author

Taryn Daniels writes sweet romance on the picturesque shores of Nantucket Island.

Aside from tending to her fluffy fur babies and being a mom-taxi, Taryn can be found daydreaming about awkward situations and swoon-worthy moments to delight her readers.

Read more at https://books.bookfunnel.com/cousinsofnantucket.